'Are you sure you can handle it?'

Gil's retort sounded suspiciously like a challenge to Olivia. 'Of course,' she replied, taking the proffered keys. Even through the glove's thickness, Olivia felt a ripple of electricity tingle along her arm. It shocked her. Five years, five long years since their last embrace yet some deep-rooted memory stirred within. She might have tried to forget but her body hadn't...couldn't...forget this man's power over her.

Dear Reader

This month, I would like to ask you to think about the kind of heroine you would like to find in our stories. Do you think she should be sweet and gentle, on the look-out for a man who will be able to care for and nurture her, or should the heroine be able to give as good as she gets, throwing punch for punch, and quite capable of standing up for herself? If you have any opinions on this matter please let us know, so that we can continue to give you the books you want to read!

The Editor

Liza Hadley gained a degree in English and European Literature and subsequently worked as both a social worker and a teacher before 'discovering' her real love—writing. Happily married with two sons, a large dog, two cats, and a pet sheep, none of whom are particularly biddable, she thoroughly enjoys being able to create characters who, at least some of the time, behave as she wants them to. Living near the Lake District, her hobbies include walking and reading.

WILLING
OR NOT

BY

LIZA HADLEY

MILLS & BOON LIMITED
ETON HOUSE, 18-24 PARADISE ROAD
RICHMOND, SURREY TW9 1SR

First published in Great Britain 1993
by Mills & Boon Limited

© Liza Hadley 1993

Australian copyright 1993
Philippine copyright 1993
This edition 1993

ISBN 0 263 78180 1

Set in Times Roman 11½ on 12 pt.
01-9308-48114 C

Made and printed in Great Britain

CHAPTER ONE

OLIVIA took her eyes off the computer screen to glance at her watch. Good heavens! Was that the time? Two o'clock. She had to be at the solicitor's office at three.

Hurriedly she skimmed through the last few paragraphs of the report with a practised eye, searching for any errors. Finding none, she printed it out and then inserted the papers into a folder entitled 'Luminar Contract'.

With one hand she tugged a comb through shoulder-length auburn curls and with the other flicked the intercom switch on her desk. 'Susan, the Luminar portfolio is ready.'

'OK, I'll be in to collect it in just a minute,' her secretary's voice sounded through the speaker.

It was a bitter February day and snowing heavily. As she reached for her coat, Olivia glanced briefly out of the window at the ever-whitening street scene below.

Her fingers froze in the middle of fastening a button as one figure in particular caught her eye. A man striding along the pavement, snowflakes catching on the thick blackness of his hair. It couldn't be... Olivia moved closer to the plate glass and stared out, but the tall, dark figure had already disappeared from sight.

She shook her head and turned back into the familiar warmth of her office, fingers trembling as she tried to secure the button. For one moment she'd actually thought it was Gil. Crazy notion! What would Gil be doing in London...in England even? Common sense told her it was impossible but couldn't quite still the painful hammering of her heart.

'I'll get that portfolio sent to—— Hey! Are you OK? You're as white as a sheet,' Susan broke off in concern as she bustled into the office.

'I thought...' Olivia paused on a shallow breath. What could she say? She thought she'd just seen a ghost from the past? Unconsciously she turned up the collar of her coat, shivering despite the central heating.

'You're worrying about this afternoon, aren't you?' Susan supplied sympathetically.

Olivia hated deceit but she couldn't explain about Gil, not even to Susan. Pushing his disturbing image firmly to the back of her mind, she nodded. Concern about the afternoon's meeting wasn't strictly responsible for her sudden pallor but wasn't a lie either. She *was* anxious about attending the reading of her grandmother's will.

The funeral had taken place nearly three weeks ago and she'd never expected such a long delay before the reading. After all, she was her grandmother's nearest relative and, as far as she knew, the estate's main beneficiary. It wasn't greed which prompted her concern, simply a desire for the legal formalities to be over and done with.

Twice already the reading had been postponed. 'Nothing serious, just one or two legal loose ends to tie up,' her grandmother's solicitor had offered in vague apology for the delay. He evidently intended the explanation to be reassuring but Olivia had received it with faint unease. Vivien Beaufort had always prided herself on her efficiency and organisational skills; 'loose ends' of any sort would have been quite out of character.

'I'm sure it won't be the ordeal you expect.' Susan gave her a reassuring smile.

'I hope you're right,' Olivia agreed.

Susan waved the sheet of paper she was holding in her hand. 'You might like to read this before you go.'

'What is it?'

'Memo to all staff informing them of Edward McKay's retirement.'

'What?' Olivia took the proffered sheet and scanned through it rapidly.

'I thought you'd be interested.'

That was an understatement. Edward McKay had been managing director of Beaufort's, the advertising agency founded by Olivia's great-grandfather, for as long as she could remember. Too long in her opinion. It was time someone younger took over.

'Who's going to replace him?' That was the crucial question.

Susan shrugged. 'Don't ask me. There's plenty of rumours buzzing on the grapevine but no official announcement yet.'

'It must be a well-guarded secret.' The office grapevine was normally a highly efficient source of information. Olivia frowned, wishing she had some idea who the new managing director would be. Beaufort's was a public company now but, as the only family member left on the staff, she felt a deep sense of responsibility for its future and wanted to be sure it was in capable hands.

The icy roads should have engaged all Olivia's attention but somehow her thoughts kept darting off in different directions. The will...Beaufort's new managing director...and, most distracting of all, Gil.

Thinking she had seen him was absurd, of course. Gil lived and worked in America. She knew it *couldn't* have been him but for those few moments back there in her office her pulse had gone into overdrive. She'd felt like a naïve eighteen-year-old again, full of adolescent turmoil and mixed-up feelings. Five long years since she'd seen him yet it might as well have been five days. Painful memories of that last humiliating encounter had resurfaced as fresh as ever. It was frightening to think that just a fleeting glimpse of a stranger could affect her so deeply. What on earth would it be like if she *were* ever to meet him again?

Olivia took a tighter grip on the steering-wheel. She had other, more important things to think about right now than imaginary sightings of Gil. He was thousands of miles away while the will and Beaufort's new managing director were problems which needed her attention now.

She was the last to arrive at the solicitor's office, and quickly took her place among the other beneficiaries, most of them friends or employees of her late grandmother. Henry Eliot fussed with the papers on his desk for several minutes, waiting for everyone to settle, before clearing his throat and starting to speak in low, ponderous tones.

Vivien would have found all this tedious in the extreme, Olivia reflected nearly half an hour later, as Henry Eliot's long, rambling monologue showed no sign of a break. Her grandmother had never had much time for sentimental speeches. She'd been a fair woman but a hard one, not given to displays of warmth or affection.

Olivia had only been ten when both her parents had died in a car accident and Vivien had taken over the role of guardian. It hadn't been easy for either of them to adjust to a new way of life; Olivia had felt the loss of her parents deeply and Vivien, in her mid-fifties, had the unexpected responsibility of a child thrust upon her. In the ensuing years, boarding-school had largely provided the means for Olivia's physical welfare while Vivien, in her reserved fashion, had done her best to provide some family warmth during the holiday periods.

It had been a somewhat austere upbringing and Olivia sometimes wondered if it was the reason why she had fallen for Gil so swiftly and so intensely. She had, quite simply, needed someone to love and be loved by. Whatever the reason, the experience had taught her a hard lesson and she hadn't made the mistake of losing her heart to any man since.

With a frown, Olivia brought her attention back to the present. Her wandering thoughts seemed somehow disrespectful. It was true that she and her grandmother had had their differences but over the years a mutual fondness and respect had developed between them and she had been genuinely saddened by her death.

'''And now to my beloved granddaughter, Olivia, I devise and bequeath all my estate both real and personal whatsoever and wheresoever...'''

There followed a list of her grandmother's possessions: the London apartment, the house in Scotland, the valuable collections of paintings and jewellery. No one hearing the details could fail to realise that Olivia Beaufort had just become a very wealthy young woman. But Olivia had never been unduly impressed by money and possessions and she heard the details now without any sense of material pleasure. She'd already learned that wealth and belongings meant little without a sense of personal fulfilment to accompany them.

Thus, only when Henry Eliot got to the very last item did her eyes betray a flicker of interest. A noise, like the sound of a door clicking open, came from the back of the room and she had to strain forward in her seat to hear properly.

''' ... and finally my shares in Beaufort's Advertising Agency.'''

Olivia breathed an unconscious sigh of relief. The shares represented a century of family history, the business which three generations of Beauforts had worked to build. Ever since she was a little girl she'd wanted to be part of that tradition and, after graduating from college two years ago, she'd worked long and hard to establish herself within the agency.

Too hard, friends told her sometimes. Her long working hours left little time for personal relationships, especially those with the opposite sex. But Olivia had had her fingers burned once and she wasn't going to risk it happening again. She felt far safer creating abstract images for the media than she did dealing with flesh-and-blood men.

But hard work wasn't just a protective screen to hide behind. She was ambitious too. The shares would entitle her to the seat on the board customarily occupied by a Beaufort and give her more influence on decision-making at a senior level.

A pause seemed to indicate that Henry Eliot had finally ended his monologue but he only gave a small, nervous cough before speaking again.

'"I bequeath the shares to Olivia on one condition. And that condition is that, until she reaches the occasion of her twenty-fifth birthday, she should work as personal assistant to the managing director of Beaufort's, in whatever capacity will enable her to become familiar with the intricacies of the advertising business at the level necessary for her to eventually take on a full and responsible role in the management, direction and leadership of the agency. Then, and only then, will the shares pass in entirety to my granddaughter and entitle her to a seat on the board of directors.'''

'What?' Olivia almost sprang out of her seat. She couldn't believe what she was hearing. It had to be a mistake. Vivien had never told her that she must serve some sort of *apprenticeship* before inheriting the shares in full.

She was immediately conscious of every eye in the room turning in her direction. After the polite smiles and patient silence which had previously accompanied the reading, her shocked outburst had all the impact of a pistol shot.

The solicitor's last words were a meaningless jumble to her and it was only when she registered a shuffling of feet and scraping of chairs that she realised the reading was finally over and that people were beginning to drift into small groups in preparation for their departure. Weather conditions were worsening by the minute and most were eager to make their farewells and leave. Even so, an interminable period of time seemed to elapse while she numbly shook hands and turned her cheek to receive assorted pecks of sympathy and affection before the last stragglers drifted away.

'If you'll excuse me, Miss Beaufort, I have to get those papers which you need to sign,' Henry Eliot murmured.

'Just a minute. I must talk to you. That clause in my grandmother's will...' But Henry Eliot had already slipped through the door into the adjoining office, evidently not at all eager to face her questions.

Hats were an unfamiliar accessory to Olivia and she removed hers now, allowing the wild tangle of auburn curls which had been reluctantly tamed by the hat's close fit to make their escape and tumble freely over her shoulders.

She arched her head backwards, exposing the graceful arc of her throat and rubbing the taut muscles at the back of her neck which seemed to have knotted in tension. Why hadn't her grandmother told her about that condition...prepared her in some way? And why had she felt it necessary to include it at all?

She was vaguely aware of a movement from the back of the room and turned carelessly, her thoughts preoccupied, then had to grasp a chairback for support as both knees almost buckled beneath her. Leaning against the door-jamb was Gil Rossaro.

With horror she discovered her ghost from the past materialised in front of her. No ethereal spirit, this, every inch of him much too solidly flesh-and-blood male. He hadn't been here when she arrived; she was sure of that. She couldn't have missed him.

Tall, with raven hair and deep olive skin, Gil bore the unmistakable stamp of his South American parentage. Deep brown eyes beneath thick level brows stared back at her now, their black depths cool and unsmiling. The features were as strikingly angled as ever, she noted, seeing the proud, arrogant look she remembered so well. Yet he was still the most attractive man she had ever seen, Olivia realised on a pang of dismay.

It *was* him she'd seen from her office window; she was sure of that now. Her body had instinctively recognised him, however much her rational mind had sought to deny it.

'How... how long have you been there?' she demanded, stumbling over the words.

'Long enough,' came the succinct response.

She recalled the noise she'd heard earlier, of a door-catch clicking. Was that when he'd arrived? Just in time to hear the details of her inheritance being read out—and her shocked outburst? The thought appalled her.

'You've no business being here at all,' she blurted out, suddenly feeling very afraid and vulnerable. The last time she'd met Gil, he'd turned her world upside-down. Was it just coincidence that he had appeared when it was on the tilt again?

However, her hostile statement merely drew a repressive look from Gil. 'I see your manners have not improved since our last meeting, Olivia. I have every right to be here. After all, I'm hardly a stranger. Have you forgotten that Vivien and I were related too, *little cousin*?'

That 'little' stung, intentionally so. Gil's sardonic tone made it clear that it wasn't any kind of familial endearment. It was the same term he'd used five years ago and it had been wholly inappropriate then—in every sense, not least its most literal. Olivia drew herself up to her full height. She'd forgotten nothing; not one moment of that long-ago summer had been erased from her memory.

At eighteen she'd been five foot eight inches tall and had considered herself fully grown in every sense of the word. Gil's teasing nickname, 'little cousin', had mocked not only her height but all her youthful attempts at adult status. How she had longed to impress him with her grown-up sophistication. How hard she'd tried to make him see the woman behind the girlish façade. Above all, though, she'd wanted him to love her.

Hurtful, jagged memories turned Olivia's eyes to glacial emeralds. Did this man know how much pain he'd caused her? No, of course he didn't, and she must never let him guess the truth.

'You may have been related to Vivien by marriage but you weren't mentioned in her will so you've no right to be here,' she insisted, chin tilting defiantly.

'Not directly mentioned, maybe, but I think I can claim to be an interested party.'

The smooth assurance behind the words made Olivia uneasy. An unease that wasn't lessened when Gil, with a leisurely thrust, stood upright and moved towards her. She wondered if it was just the expensive cut of his clothes which gave that fluid ease to his movements.

A dark cashmere coat accentuated the broad span of his shoulders while a polo-necked sweater clung to a lean, muscle-hardened torso. Gil was only about six inches taller than her but somehow she felt dwarfed by·him. He had changed, she acknowledged. Five years had toughened and honed Gil's maleness to rugged perfection. Was this what she had been afraid of—that time would not lessen but intensify his appeal? Was that why she had been so strenuously determined to avoid him in all this time?

The unpalatable answers to those questions caused a blush to make its way all the way from Olivia's throat to her cheeks, making her redhead's pale skin flame with colour. 'It's much too hot in here,' she mumbled desperately, in a feeble attempt to explain away her heated flush.

'You're not about to faint, are you?' Gil's drawled question implied not the least concern if she was.

Olivia closed her eyes, as if to protect herself from his indifference. 'Don't worry,' she assured him. 'I've never fainted in my life and I'm not about to start now.'

'I'm glad to hear it. A histrionic tendency is not a quality I look for in my personal assistants.'

'What——?' Olivia gazed at him, only half registering the implication of his words.

Knowing he had her full attention, Gil's gaze held hers mercilessly for several seconds. 'I don't believe you know that I was appointed managing director of Beaufort's yesterday.'

The icy cold which gripped Olivia had nothing to do with the weather outdoors. 'What are you talking about?' she whispered.

Gil's shrug was infuriatingly casual. 'Edward McKay has been wanting to retire for some time and Vivien's death prompted him into finally making the decision. The board offered me the job and I accepted.'

'Just like that?'

'Just . . . like . . . that . . . yes.' The curt precision of each word allowed no room for doubt.

'But how...how could they possibly make such a decision...so hastily...without even consulting the shareholders?' Her mind groped for reasons to deny it.

'I think the board regarded their action as decisive rather than hasty. It was a unanimous decision which will, of course, have to be ratified at the next general meeting of the shareholders. The board do not anticipate any objections.'

Probably not! No doubt most of the shareholders would consider it quite a *coup* that the board had somehow managed to acquire the services of a man who already owned one of New York's biggest and most prestigious advertising agencies. Beaufort's had a respectable client list but it was small fry compared with Rossaro Advertising.

It was easy enough to see why the board had approached Gil with such an offer but it was not so easy to understand why Gil had accepted it. Why, she wondered dazedly, had he taken the job? What possible interest could Beaufort's hold for him?

'But...but you live in New York. How can you be managing director of Beaufort's?' she said weakly.

Gil gave a low, amused laugh. 'The world is becoming a smaller place every day, Olivia. It's easy enough to travel between New York and London. Besides, I have a perfectly good deputy who can run Rossaro's for the time being. I plan to settle in London for a while.'

Settle in London? Evidently this wasn't just a token appointment. Gil *was* going to be based at

Beaufort's. Olivia's heart seemed to skip a beat
as she realised what that would mean for her.
'So... so it's all finalised, then?'

'Down to the last detail.'

Olivia's mind reeled. Learning of the condition in Vivien's will was bad enough but discovering that Gil would be moving to London
and that she would be expected to work for him
was horrifying.

'When... when was all this decided?'

'A couple of weeks ago.'

A couple of weeks ago? Pieces of a jigsaw
slotted together in Olivia's mind. She recalled
Henry Eliot's evasive telephone call informing her
about the postponement. 'Your appointment was
the reason for the reading being delayed, wasn't
it?' she demanded shakily.

Gil shrugged. 'I contacted Henry Eliot and
suggested he postpone the reading until my appointment had been officially confirmed. In the
circumstances, I thought it best you should know
whom you would be working for from the start.'

'How thoughtful of you,' Olivia murmured
insincerely, and then the implication of his words
struck her—'know whom you would be working
for'. 'Then you must also have known about the
condition in my grandmother's will?' It was half-
accusation, half-question.

Gil sat down in one of the vacant chairs,
stretching long legs out in front of him. 'Vivien
discussed it with me, yes.'

So Vivien had talked about it to Gil but not
to her. A wave of hurt engulfed Olivia at learning
that the two of them had talked about her,

without her knowledge, let alone inclusion. She had been aware that Vivien and Gil met from time to time to discuss business but not that they were in the habit of discussing such personal matters— not that they were in the habit of discussing *her*!

It shocked her to realise to what extent Gil had manipulated events during the last few weeks, and perhaps longer. Just how often had he played puppet-master, tugging the strings of her life this way and that with an unseen hand?

She felt like a punch-drunk boxer, dazed by too many blows. She couldn't think straight. While her mind reeled from the effort of trying to assimilate so many unpleasant discoveries, Henry Eliot re-entered the room and saw Gil. 'Ah, good afternoon, Mr Rossaro. You've arrived at last. I got your message to say you would be delayed... Were the roads bad?'

Through their brief exchange of small talk, Olivia tried to gather her shattered thoughts. Surely there had to be something she could do to get out of this. There had to be a loophole somewhere. In desperation she turned to Henry Eliot.

'Is there anything I can do about that condition? To alter it, I mean?'

He looked surprised at the abrupt question. 'I don't understand. Is there...?'

'Can I alter it?' Olivia insisted.

The solicitor shook his head. 'No. It's a perfectly proper inclusion in the will and one which your grandmother was fully entitled to make.'

'But she didn't tell me about it... didn't even discuss it with me.'

'The condition was included as a safeguard,' Henry Eliot said gently. 'Your grandmother was concerned that, given your youth and inexperience, you weren't yet ready for a seat on the board. Had she lived longer... until you were a little older and had gained more experience in the advertising business... then the condition would have been removed from the will. You need never have known about it. I imagine that was why she decided not to tell you of it.'

His explanation eased some of the hurt Olivia had first felt on learning of the condition. Maybe Vivien hadn't wanted to upset her by mentioning it, perhaps unnecessarily. And, knowing Vivien's firm belief that youth and enthusiasm were no substitute for experience, Olivia could also understand her reasoning. But that didn't make the terms any easier to accept. Working for Edward McKay would have been bad enough but working for Gil would surely be impossible.

'And if I refuse to comply?' It was a last-ditch hope.

The solicitor's expression was grave. 'I'm afraid that if you refuse, or if you fail to honour the condition for the full period specified by your grandmother, then you lose all entitlement to the shares. They will immediately be transferred to Mr Rossaro here.'

So that was it. She would lose the shares and all say in the future management of the agency, at least at board level where it was most influential. Even more galling, Gil would get all the shares which were rightfully hers. They would drop straight into his lap without him even having to lift a finger. If her grandmother had wanted to ensure her compliance with the terms of the will, she couldn't have chosen a better way of doing it. Vivien had known how much the agency meant to Olivia, and that she would never voluntarily relinquish her shares in it—certainly not to Gil!

'Are you all right, Miss Beaufort? You've gone quite pale. Let me get you a glass of water.' Henry Eliot filled a small beaker from a jug and handed it to her.

'Thank you,' Olivia murmured, sipping the icy water.

'Feeling better now?'

Olivia nodded. 'Yes, I'm sorry...'

'Not to worry...perfectly understandable. Now, if you wouldn't mind signing these papers and then you can get along home.'

With difficulty, she brought her attention back to the sheets of buff-coloured paper which Mr Eliot was setting out in front of her. Earlier in the week they'd gone through them together, and with only a cursory glance Olivia put her signature to them now. She didn't want to prolong this meeting any longer than was necessary.

Sometimes she'd imagined what it would be like to meet Gil again, but in those dreams she'd always appeared sophisticated and poised, greeting him with cool politeness and letting it be quite clear that his 'little cousin' was fully grown at last. How different reality often proved to dreams. The shock of seeing him so unexpectedly had destroyed any pretence of composure and she couldn't disguise the disturbing

effect his presence was having on her. The control
which she prided herself on was crumbling by the
minute.

'Would you like me to call a taxi? You still
don't look too well,' Henry Eliot enquired sol-
icitously as she replaced the top of her fountain-
pen.

Olivia shook her head. 'No, my car's outside.'

'I really don't think you should be driving,'
Henry Eliot frowned.

Before Olivia could say a word, Gil had
spoken. 'I'll drive Miss Beaufort home.'

'Excellent...excellent,' the solicitor smiled,
evidently thankful that arrangements had been
taken out of his hands.

Oh, no! It was going to take all the strength
she could muster just to walk out of the office.
The thought of having to share the close confines
of a car with Gil turned her limbs to jelly.

'No, I can drive myself,' she quickly declined
the offer, unable to resist the suppressive trailer,
'I feel safer when I'm behind the wheel.
Grandmother might have needed the services of
a chauffeur but I certainly don't.'

It was a deliberate snub and they both knew
it, but Gil merely gave a cool smile. 'In that case
you can drive me. That way we will all be satisfied. Mr Eliot can be assured that you are not
travelling alone...you can be behind the
wheel...and instead it is I who have the services
of a chauffeur. You can pick up your car another
time.'

Somehow the snub had rebounded on her,
Olivia was forced to acknowledge ruefully. Damn

Gil! How had he managed to manoeuvre the situation round so skilfully? 'Your suggestion certainly seems to have solved the problem,' she murmured ungraciously.

Gil leaned forward to pick up the hat she had set down on the desk earlier, using the privacy awarded by the movement to whisper huskily, 'My job is solving... or removing... problems. You'll soon discover it's something I'm very good at, little cousin.'

CHAPTER TWO

THERE were several vehicles parked by the solicitor's office but Olivia instinctively knew which one was Gil's. The black Jaguar suited him perfectly: large, sleek and dangerous.

She stopped beside it and shivered, though whether at the thought of taking the wheel of such a powerful car or simply at the prospect of being inside it with Gil she wasn't sure.

'Changed your mind about driving?'

'No. Why should I?' she denied with a touch of bravado.

Gil eyed her over the snow-covered roof. 'I just thought you looked a little... apprehensive.'

She was apprehensive all right, but she didn't want him to guess why. She felt far too exposed already by the events of the afternoon. 'Are you sure you trust me to drive it in these road conditions?' she returned, half hoping he wouldn't.

'Are *you* sure you can handle it?'

The quickfire retort sounded suspiciously like a challenge and Olivia wasn't going to risk looking foolish by backing down. 'Of course,' she said firmly, taking the proffered keys and opening the door, triggering the release mechanism of the passenger door at the same time.

The car was by no means cramped but somehow it felt it, and Olivia was painfully aware of Gil's proximity as she fumbled with her seatbelt. All her attempts to secure it failed until Gil took her stiff, uncooperative fingers in his and pushed the metal clip firmly home.

It was the first time he had touched her and even through the glove's thickness Olivia felt a ripple of electricity tingle along her arm. It shocked her. Five years, five long years since their last embrace yet some deep-rooted memory stirred within. She might have tried to forget but her body hadn't... couldn't... forget this man's power over her.

She risked a shy glance at him from beneath her lashes. Did he feel it too? If he did there was no evidence of it in the relaxed line of his body or the smooth precision of his movements as he adjusted settings on the facia panel.

Olivia bit her lip and concentrated on inserting the key in the ignition. Don't be a fool, she chastised herself sternly. What occurred five years ago meant nothing to Gil. He's probably forgotten it even happened. How she wished she could make the same claim for herself.

Minutes later they were on the main road and Olivia, normally a confident driver, felt uncharacteristically nervous. She tried to put it down to the strange car and icy roads but knew that Gil's presence was more responsible for her anxiety than anything else. Much too conscious of his nearness, she had to force herself to concentrate on manoeuvres she would normally have performed automatically.

Finally, though, the silence became too much for her and she found herself asking, 'How long will it be before you officially take over as managing director?'

'I already have.'

The swift response took her by surprise. She'd expected, or perhaps hoped for, a respite of several weeks before Gil finally divested himself of his commitments in America. Job changes at such a senior level were not usually so easily accomplished. The board of directors must have bent over backwards to persuade him to take over so quickly.

'Already?' It was difficult not to let her disappointment show.

Gil nodded. 'Which means that from now on you'll be working for me. You can transfer your things to the office adjoining mine tomorrow.'

'From tomorrow?' Olivia's heart sank at hearing those ominous words. Everything was happening too quickly. The frightening reality of exactly how much that condition would change her life hadn't truly sunk in until now.

'But I'm in the middle of dealing with several accounts . . . I can't just abandon them.'

Gil's look held a hint of impatience. 'I'm not suggesting that you abandon them. I've already arranged for your existing client accounts to be reallocated to other executives within the department.'

'You've done what?' Olivia spluttered, suddenly angry. ''How dare you interfere with my work without even consulting me? You had no right——'

'I had every right,' Gil cut off her words with an icy blast. 'As managing director it is my responsibility to deploy staff in the jobs where I feel they can be most effective. You can't function as my assistant in the job you're doing now.'

A half-formed hope had been taking shape in her mind earlier that maybe Gil would let her keep her present job, stay where she was. But that hope was dashed now. 'You . . . you really want me to work as your assistant, then?'

'What else did you think I would be employing you as?'

'I . . . I don't know.'

'You surely didn't think I was going to keep you on as a sinecure?'

'Certainly not!' Olivia leapt hotly to her own defence. 'I'm not looking for some sort of soft option. I just didn't expect to have to work for you directly, that's all.'

'Expect, or want?' Gil demanded drily.

'All right, then, *want*,' Olivia admitted, deciding that she might as well lay all her cards on the table. 'I like my job. I don't want to have to change it. And I don't want to work for you.'

'That's frank, at least, but I'm afraid that what you want has very little to do with it,' Gil drawled. 'From now on you *will* be working for me so you'd better get used to the idea.'

Olivia felt like hitting him. If both hands hadn't been needed on the steering-wheel, she might well have given in to the temptation. Suddenly a horrible thought occurred to her. Gil could be planning to make her life so difficult under him that she would be glad to leave her job...or even be sacked. If she left, for whatever reason, he would get her shares; that's what the solicitor had said. 'How do I know you aren't planning to get rid of me just to get your hands on my shares?' she demanded.

'You don't,' Gil said bluntly. 'You'll just have to trust me. If you're good at your job, you'll have nothing to fear.'

And that was about as much reassurance as she was going to get, Olivia thought angrily. Trust Gil! She'd rather trust a rattlesnake. 'And what exactly will my work as your assistant entail?' she demanded warily.

'Assisting me, of course,' Gil said blandly.

'Doing what?'

'Several of my clients at Rossaro Advertising are planning to introduce media campaigns in this country. I intend to make sure Beaufort's wins those accounts, and you're going to help me.'

'But why can't I just continue to deal with the client accounts I have now?' That way she wouldn't have to work with Gil.

Gil's sigh indicated that he was having difficulty keeping his patience. 'Because it's time you learned to handle accounts on a bigger scale. That's the kind of experience you're going to need if you ever want to occupy that seat on the board. Besides, I think Beaufort's is ready to branch into a wider advertising market. It's been doing well enough during the last few years but not nearly as well as it could be. I plan to change that.'

Olivia didn't know if she liked what Gil was planning. Beaufort's had always prided itself on the quality of service and personal touch it could offer its clients as a smaller agency. She didn't want it to become a big, faceless agency like some of the American giants.

'Don't you think you should spend some time familiarising yourself with the company's structure before you plan any sweeping changes? Beaufort's isn't Rossaro Advertising, you know,' she suggested tersely.

Gil's gaze flicked sideways, giving her a brief glimpse of dark eyes, the deep brown iris and black pupil almost indistinguishable. 'I do know. I'm already familiar with the organisation of Beaufort's. Vivien kept me closely informed of its progress. I'm fully aware of its strengths and weaknesses, I can assure you,' he told her calmly.

Olivia gritted her teeth. Was there anything that Gil didn't know about Beaufort's—or her—thanks to Vivien?

The brief silence which followed was broken by Gil. 'I've arranged a meeting first thing tomorrow morning for all senior personnel. I think you'll have a better idea of my plans and your role in them after hearing what I've got to say then.'

'Tomorrow morning? I'll have to look in my diary but I think I'm free,' she said, perversely wanting to annoy him.

But Gil was one step ahead of her. 'I've already checked and you are,' he informed her, adding, 'Though, even if you hadn't been, this meeting would have taken priority over any other engagement.'

Olivia's fingers tensed on the steering-wheel. If she'd expected a gradual transition between finishing her present job and starting as Gil's assistant, she'd been badly mistaken. From now on Gil was her boss and he wasn't going to let her forget it. Not for one minute.

A few minutes later, she stood on the pavement outside her apartment block, watching his black Jaguar glide away. With a sinking heart, she acknowledged that there were going to be major changes at Beaufort's—affecting her more than anyone.

She'd expected changes but not this sort. This morning she'd been cautiously anticipating a seat on the board. Now she found she'd lost her job and was expected to work for a man she'd hoped never to set eyes on again. Talk about counting chickens!

Once inside her apartment, Olivia clasped her arms round herself and shivered. Despite the central heating, she felt icy cold. Reaction, she told herself firmly. To the will or to Gil? a small voice asked. She didn't know the answer.

As soon as she'd caught sight of him, her body had begun to respond, arousing senses long dormant. Dormant since... No! She wouldn't allow herself to dwell on what had happened five years ago. It was over and done with. There was no point in raking it up again. Any regrets she harboured about the adolescent behaviour she'd displayed then would simply have to remain regrets.

She felt chilled to the bone, as though her body would never feel warm again. Right at that moment, Olivia desperately wished there was someone to hold her close, warm her... love her.

The lack of someone special in her life had never felt more acute.

She stretched tensely. Maybe a bath would ease those aching muscles and warm her up a little, physically at least.

After discarding her clothes randomly across the bathroom floor, Olivia sank down into the big circular tub and closed her eyes. Mmm . . . what bliss! For a while she could forget everything, even . . . especially . . . Gil.

But somehow Olivia discovered that Gil's image was as difficult to ignore as the man himself. No matter how many times she tried to focus her thoughts on to some more pleasantly distracting topic, he kept reappearing, refusing to be dismissed. In the end the effort to banish him proved impossible and Olivia reluctantly accepted his intrusion. Perhaps if she just allowed her mind to follow its own inclinations, it would prove therapeutic. Exorcise him once and for all.

Inevitably her thoughts drifted back to the summer five years ago when she had returned to London for the summer holidays. She'd just completed her final year at boarding-school and the prospect of starting at college in the autumn was both exciting and frightening. Accustomed to the sheltered regime of an all-girl school, she'd been looking forward to the freedom of college, but was also a little apprehensive about coping with the independence it would offer.

She'd received the news that Gil Rossaro, the stepcousin she had never met, was in London with only mild curiosity. Her mind had been too full of her own future plans to allow much room for anything else.

She supposed Philip, Gil's late stepfather, was the closest to a skeleton in the cupboard that the Beaufort family had known, at least in recent history. Oliver Beaufort, her grandfather, had always hoped that both his sons, Philip and Olivia's father, William, would follow him into the family advertising agency. William had done so willingly but Philip was more at home in the country than the city and had no enthusiasm for business. After numerous family arguments on the subject he had emigrated instead to South America. His decision had created a rift between father and son which was never healed, and Oliver had cut Philip out of his life completely.

None the less Philip had prospered: he married a wealthy Argentinian widow and successfully turned his talents to ranching. There were no children from the marriage but Philip's wife had a son, Gil, by her first husband.

It seemed that Gil had acquired the taste for business which had eluded his stepfather and, after Harvard, had started his own advertising agency in New York. It grew quickly and acquired an impressive reputation within a few years, soon becoming one of Madison Avenue's biggest and most respected agencies.

Gil's trip to England was prompted mainly by business interests but he had decided to use the opportunity to meet Vivien and Olivia for the first time.

That first meeting! Olivia recalled it so vividly that just thinking about it seemed to wipe away the last five years and transform her once again into an eighteen-year-old teenager, fresh out of school and still uncertain of how to deal with adults, men in particular.

'Olivia, this is Gil Rossaro,' her grandmother had introduced him on the first evening home.

Shyly Olivia had shaken his hand, feeling her own palm grow suddenly moist as she gazed into Gil's eyes for the first time.

Expecting to meet a dull executive type, she had instead found herself face to face with the sort of rugged physique and dark, brooding good looks she had thought only existed in romantic novels. She had been totally unprepared for the tidal wave of emotion which had swept through her and almost bowled her over. He was, she had decided instantly, the most attractive man she had ever met.

And the most fascinating, she had discovered over dinner. Until then, her contact with the opposite sex had been mainly limited to the brothers of friends. Gil, some ten years older, was her first real encounter with a mature man, an intriguing mixture of urbane sophistication and virile masculinity. It was an irresistible combination and his dry wit and amusing conversation had held her spellbound throughout the meal.

Too self-conscious to make more than briefly murmured contributions at the dinner table, Olivia was thrown completely when Vivien suggested, 'Why don't you take Gil to visit some of the city sights one day this week?'

Olivia felt herself blushing furiously. 'He...he wouldn't be interested,' she protested, certain that a man of Gil's sophisticated tastes would have no enthusiasm for the usual tourist trail of attractions and monuments.

'Who says?' he said with gentle teasing, as if sensing her discomfort and trying to put her at her ease. 'I've only been waiting for the right guide.'

Olivia stared at him. 'You really mean it? You'd really like to go?' she burst out, hardly knowing whether to be elated or terrified at the prospect of spending a whole day in his company.

'I'd really like to go,' he assured her, smiling.

'All right, then,' Olivia agreed, returning his smile and trying to still the tremor of delight which filled her.

On the chosen day, she was up well before six o'clock and had already changed her clothes half a dozen times before breakfast. She had dismissed half her wardrobe as too schoolgirlish and the other half as too formal. She wanted to look casually elegant, but no matter how many times she mixed and matched her clothes nothing seemed to look right. In the end she decided on white cotton trousers coupled with a smart navy and white sailor-style top. It wasn't quite the effect she wanted but it was the best she could do.

Breakfast was a waste of time. She couldn't eat a thing. Her stomach felt as tense as it had done when she was sitting exams and she could hardly wait for Gil to arrive so that they could be on their way.

When she heard his knock on the front door, her heart started to beat like a jungle drum. What

on earth would they talk about? she wondered
in sudden panic. What did it matter? her heart
responded. Even if they didn't exchange a single
word, just being with him would be enough.

But in the event she needn't have worried. To
begin with Gil did most of the talking, making
her laugh by recounting some amusing anecdotes
from the world of advertising. But he proved to
be a good listener too and before long Olivia
found herself telling him things she hadn't been
able to discuss with anyone before: the loss of
her parents, anxieties about college, career plans,
hopes and dreams for the future.

The day seemed to go by all too quickly as they
took in the Tower of London, Buckingham
Palace, St Paul's Cathedral and Westminster
Abbey, until, by late afternoon, they were at
Hampton Court, laughing as they tried to find
their way out of its famous maze.

'I thought you said you'd done this before,'
Gil mocked as they found themselves at yet
another dead end.

'I didn't say how long it had taken me,' Olivia
giggled.

'Let me try this time,' Gil suggested, taking
her hand to lead her back down the route they
had just followed.

It was the first time they had shared more than
a fleeting physical contact, and when his hand
touched hers Olivia felt as if she'd just received
a massive jolt of electricity. It shot through her
whole body, almost pinning her feet to the
ground. She could hardly believe the violence of
her reaction.

Her shock must have communicated itself to Gil because he turned round, his dark gaze narrowing on her face.

'Are you all right?'

No, of course she wasn't all right. She'd never felt like this before, never known it was possible to feel such a fierce longing for something she couldn't name...didn't even understand. But she couldn't say any of that to Gil, so she nodded weakly and tried to smile. 'I...I just stumbled,' she murmured.

'Are you getting tired?'

She shook her head. 'No, I'm fine.'

For some reason Gil was still holding her hand and he was looking at her strangely. 'How long did you say it took you to get out of here last time?' he asked softly.

Olivia felt her mouth go dry and the blood seemed to be pounding through her head. 'About a week, I think,' she attempted to joke.

Gil's pupils suddenly seemed very black. 'Well, I don't think it would be a good idea for us to be stuck in here that long this time,' he said drily. 'Come on, follow me.' And he swung round, abruptly dropping her hand.

Olivia stared after him. She couldn't explain it, didn't know how it had happened, but in that instant she knew beyond any doubt that she had fallen in love with Gil. She didn't care if they remained trapped in the maze forever. All she knew was that she wanted to be with Gil and never, ever to leave him.

At home, later, she stared at herself in the mirror. Why don't I look different? she demanded of herself. She felt so different that it seemed impossible that her outer appearance hadn't changed too. The schoolgirl of only a couple of weeks ago had gone forever and in her place was a woman, a woman who had suddenly learned the wildly sweet delight of knowing herself in love.

The next few days were the most wonderful Olivia had ever known. Her life revolved around Gil's visits, which became more frequent as her grandmother increasingly sought his advice on company affairs. It was obvious that Vivien trusted his judgement and for the first time Olivia realised just how much her grandmother, for all her sternly independent exterior, must have missed the guiding hands of her husband and eldest son.

'I shall miss Gil when he goes back to New York,' Vivien said one morning at breakfast.

Olivia stared at her. 'What did you say?' she demanded.

Vivien's eyes narrowed at the sharp edge to the question. 'I said I shall miss Gil,' she repeated a little stiffly.

'I . . . I didn't know he was leaving.'

'He has his own business to run, Olivia. He's already extended his visit longer than he intended.'

Reality had no place in Olivia's romantic daydreams and she felt its intrusion now with a painful thrust. Somewhere in the back of her mind she supposed she had known that Gil must return to New York, but she'd pushed it aside, focusing all her thoughts on each day's visit and cherishing every exchange between them, however brief.

'When...when is he going?' she asked numbly.

'Quite soon. Sunday or Monday, I think,' Vivien said, getting up from the table.

A knife seemed to twist in Olivia's heart. She loved Gil and she couldn't bear the thought of him returning to America and leaving her. Surely if he knew how she felt about him he would offer to take her with him? She could go to college in America...she could work for Gil's agency. There were a hundred possibilities. If only she could find a way of letting him know how she felt.

Inadvertently it was Vivien who provided her with the perfect opportunity. Olivia had been invited to a twenty-first birthday party at the weekend and had already decided that she couldn't possibly go, not with Gil's departure so close, when Vivien suggested that she take Gil too.

'I'm sure he'd enjoy it and, besides, I'll be away myself on Saturday night so I'd be relieved to know you were in good hands and had someone to ensure you got home safely.'

Tentatively Olivia asked Gil, and when he agreed it was difficult for her to contain her delight. It was a heaven-sent opportunity, a chance to show Gil the woman she could be. A woman who loved him and who, she hardly dared voice the hope aloud, desperately wanted him to love her in return. Surely when he saw her in a more sophisticated setting he would realise that she was much more to him than just his 'little cousin'?

As soon as her grandmother left for her engagement on Saturday afternoon, Olivia set her plan into action. She had already decided that nothing in her wardrobe was suitable for such an important occasion and that a new outfit was necessary. Within half an hour, she was in the city's West End, scouring its boutiques.

When she surveyed herself in the mirror that evening, Olivia hardly recognised the strikingly made-up female who stared back at her. The short black dress clung to the budding curves of hip and breasts and swooped low at the back, making it very obvious that she wasn't wearing a bra. Newly washed hair billowed round her shoulders in an auburn cloud, creating just the sort of wild look that Olivia wanted. Bright red lipstick made a pouting Cupid's bow of her lips, startling against her pale skin.

When she entered the drawing-room, Gil was already there. He glanced up briefly from the paper he was reading and Olivia saw his dark gaze flick over her once and then again, not quite so fleetingly. Good! At last she had his attention.

'Is that what you're wearing to the party?' he demanded, eyes narrowing.

Olivia nodded and twirled provocatively. 'Like it?'

'No,' came the curt response.

For a moment Olivia was nonplussed by the blatant put-down, so different was this Gil from the gently mocking figure she had grown accustomed to.

'You're not used to seeing me dressed up, that's all,' she retorted, tilting her chin with a touch of defiance. Until now Gil had seen her mainly in the comfortable jeans which were her normal holiday attire, and even if he had seen her in a more dressy outfit it certainly hadn't been anything like this—her grandmother would never have permitted it.

'Has Vivien seen you in that dress?' Gil demanded, as if guessing the direction of her thoughts.

Fearful that he might get all high-handed and order her to change if she admitted not, Olivia crossed her fingers behind her back and nodded. 'It's not what she would choose to wear herself, of course, but——'

The rest of the sentence was snapped off as Gil set aside his paper with an angry thud. 'But she permits her granddaughter to dress like a tart? Don't lie to me, Olivia!'

Dismay at what Gil might disclose to Vivien combined with a sharp sense of hurt at his tersely delivered insult. Olivia had chosen the dress especially to please Gil yet, far from liking it, he'd seemed to find it in some way objectionable. She bristled defensively. 'Believe what you like. This is what I'm wearing to the party whether you approve or not.'

In one swift movement Gil stood upright. 'And if I refuse to take you?'

'I'll call a taxi.'

For several seconds their eyes locked in silent combat and when Gil's eyes left hers Olivia believed fleetingly that she had won. But Gil's gaze merely descended, with such leisurely insolence that Olivia felt every curve of her body come under his scrutiny. Almost simultaneously the heat of anger faded to be replaced by an icy cold, and then that too was gone and in its place came heat again, but different this time, its origins in deep, secret, unfamiliar places.

'Stop it!' she demanded, shocked to hear the shrill edge to her voice. Gil's eyes held hers once more.

'Don't you like it?' he demanded with mocking insolence.

'No!'

'Well, if you wear that dress tonight, sweetheart, you're going to attract a hell of a lot more looks like it.'

All the uncertainty of her youth flooded in on Olivia. She didn't want to attract lots of male attention, only Gil's. Yet she didn't want him looking at her like this either. Or did she? One moment she wanted her safe, amusing holiday companion back again, the next this dark, unknown stranger who provoked such strange, exciting sensations.

Confusion welled up in her. What did she want? She didn't know. But acceding to Gil's demand that she change her dress smacked of defeat, of retreating back into the safe childhood world she had inhabited until now. She didn't want to play safe. She didn't want to be a child any longer and she certainly didn't want to be treated like one. In a moment of impulsive rebellion, Olivia made her decision.

'I don't care how men look at me. I'm wearing it to please myself, not them,' she retorted defiantly.

'If you were ten years older, I might just believe you.'

Olivia had been about to make some indignant
retort but Gil held up his hand in a silencing
gesture. 'Spare me the aggravation, Olivia. I've
said all I've got to say on the subject. Wear what
you like.'

It should have felt like a victory, albeit a petty
one, but it didn't. It felt as if Gil had abruptly
lost interest in her, as if she'd somehow disappointed him. Olivia tried to summon a sense of
triumph to combat the feeling of deflation his
words had produced, and failed miserably.

They didn't speak throughout the journey to
the party. Olivia longed to say something to re-
store their previous ease in each other's company
but didn't know what or how. She hoped Gil
might relent and extend some kind of olive-
branch but the harsh angles of his profile never
relaxed once.

At the party, Olivia immediately threw herself
into the dancing, determined that Gil should not
realise how much their disagreement had upset
her. Unaccustomed to alcohol, she none the less
downed a couple of glasses of wine in quick suc-
cession. Their effect, combined with the heady
realisation that her 'new look' was attracting
more than a fair share of male attention, made
her behaviour uncharacteristically exhibition-
istic. Her laugh grew more giggly, her dancing
more daring and her behaviour more flirtatious
with every passing minute. Yet it was always Gil
her eyes sought out in the crowd, determined that

he should see what a good time she was having despite his earlier disapproval.

But when she realised that Gil's attention was no longer on her but was engaged, very thoroughly, by a sylph-like blonde, she was unprepared for the blow of jealousy which hit her deep in the pit of her stomach.

When her dancing partner suggested they go outside for a few minutes to cool down, she agreed readily, only aware that she could not bear the sight of Gil and another woman together for even a second longer.

Once outside, however, and having led Olivia to one of the screened arbours in the garden, Andrew made it clear that cooling down was the last thing on his mind. His kiss had taken Olivia by surprise and, when her befuddled senses made her somewhat slow in resisting, he took her lack of protest as encouragement to further liberties. Before she'd registered what was happening, the flimsy bodice of her dress was descending with horrifying speed.

The next few moments were a confused nightmare in Olivia's mind. Before she had a chance to do anything herself, she was aware of Andrew's body being hauled off hers with powerful ease and of Gil imposing himself between the two of them, his face a rigid mask of anger.

'What the hell do you two think you're doing?' he demanded, harsh condemnation separating each word and endowing it with a steel tip.

'I don't see that it's any of your——'

'Shut up.' Gil peremptorily cut off Andrew's blustering attempt at bravado.

Andrew took one look at Gil's set features and instantly complied with the instruction.

'Well?' Gil fixed Olivia with an icy glare.

'We...I...' Olivia stumbled over the words, fervently wishing the ground would open up and swallow her. She was acutely conscious of Gil's hawk-like scrutiny taking in every flickering expression on her face and, much worse, every inch of newly exposed flesh on the upper curves of her breasts.

'You can go.' With a jerk of his head, Gil dismissed Andrew, who, with evident relief, promptly did as he was told.

'Well? I'm still waiting for some sort of explanation.'

The sardonic drawl made it clear that there wasn't going to be any similar reprieve for Olivia.

Gil stood in front of her, a towering monolith against the black sky and just as granite-like. Unconsciously Olivia moistened her lips, unaware of the sensuality in the simple action. 'Nothing...nothing really happened.'

'Do you call this nothing?' His gaze ranged downwards over her dishevelled clothing. 'A man gets as far as nearly removing your dress and you call it nothing?'

Olivia wanted to look away, to escape from the wrath, which was almost a physical assault, that she saw in his eyes, but their black depths held hers like a magnet. 'He...he didn't nearly remove my...my dress,' she stammered, struggling to pull it back into place with numb, uncooperative fingers.

A contemptuous rumble sounded in Gil's throat. 'He was doing a pretty good job from where I was standing.'

She tried to say something, to defend herself, but no sounds would come. Her throat felt parched, as though all the moisture had been drained from it.

For some reason Gil seemed to find her silence more inflammatory than any words might have been. 'What does it take to score higher than a zero on your rating scale? Is this *nothing*?'

The next moment he was pulling her against him until her breasts flattened against his chest, their sensitive flesh stimulated by the bristling bed of hairs they encountered through the fine material of his shirt. Then his mouth was on hers, plundering its softness with a fierce, angry possession which made no allowance for her youth and inexperience.

Yet even if she'd wanted to protest Olivia knew she couldn't have done so. Gil's kiss stilled every tiny shred of resistance so that soon she was filled with a languid warmth which knew only acceptance. Her thoughts veered off into dizzying spirals, swallowed up in the velvety blackness which enveloped her while her body delighted in the alien sensations which engulfed her.

Why had no one told her it would be like this? Why had nothing prepared her for such sweet, exhilarating feelings?

Finally Gil dragged his mouth from hers to graze a path to the upturned curve of her throat.

Totally bemused, Olivia arched her neck willingly and offered him access to the quivering pulse which beat there.

'Do you called that *nothing*?' he repeated thickly against her skin.

Mutely Olivia shook her head. How could she deny it when there was a world of difference between what Andrew had done and the sensations Gil had aroused? It was like comparing coarse apple cider with the purest champagne. Only how could you know the difference until you'd had a chance to try both?

'This is crazy,' Gil muttered roughly. 'You're only a child.'

Olivia had never felt less childlike. She was a woman in love and her body glowed with feminine awareness. She didn't want these wonderful, delicious sensations to end. She wanted them to go on forever and ever. She wanted Gil to love her forever. Desperately her fingers curled into the silky material of his shirt. 'Andrew didn't think I was a child,' she whispered.

'Andrew didn't care!'

Did that mean Gil did—care for her? Was Gil about to tell her he loved her? He had to be. Olivia felt her heart do something resembling a somersault. 'And you do?'

There was a brief silence before Gil spoke and when he did there was a guarded edge to his voice. 'I care about not violating Vivien's trust . . . and about the fact that although you may be legally of age you're still too young for this sort of grown-up game.'

Disappointment coursed through Olivia. Naïvely she'd hoped for a declaration of love and had been reminded instead that in Gil's eyes she was still only his little cousin. The intimacy they had shared only moments ago was slipping away and she longed desperately to revive it. But how? How could she convince Gil she wasn't a child but a grown woman—a woman who loved him, who only wanted him to love her in return? 'I'm...I'm not too young,' she murmured softly.

'Not in years maybe but, in terms of experience, yes, you are too young,' Gil insisted huskily.

Guided only by the force of her feelings and not thinking where her reckless words might lead her, Olivia rushed headlong into them. 'I'm not as inexperienced as you seem to think.'

She got no further before Gil's hands came up to grip her bare shoulders. 'What the hell are you trying to say?' he demanded, eyes blazing warningly.

Shocked both by his abrupt change in tone and by the painful bite of his nails into her flesh, Olivia stuttered, 'I—I...'

'My God! And I thought that lout was taking advantage of you. But you were with him all the way, weren't you? This isn't anything new to you, is it?' Gil looked as if he wanted to hit her. 'Good God! Just how many men have you slept with, you little tramp?'

Stunned by his furious response and by the unexpected demands, Olivia could only stare at him in horrified silence. All at once she knew she'd gone too far. Much too far. In her desperate wish for Gil to treat her as a woman, she had blundered on blindly, never imagining the incensed reaction it would produce. She had to tell him the truth. Anything was better than having him look at her with such burning contempt in his expression. 'I——'

But before she could get any further Gil interrupted her, his voice as taut as a whiplash. 'Spare me the details, Olivia; I'm not interested. Now get your bag. I'm taking you home.'

The journey home was as silent as the outward one had been. Olivia sat curled up in the passenger-seat, hugging her pain and misery to herself like a cloak. She felt humiliated and soiled; the dress which had seemed so glamorous now showed itself to be cheap and tawdry. All the hopes which had filled her head when she had bought it had been shattered like fragile glass. Life would never, ever be the same again.

When the car drew to a halt outside her grandmother's, she remained huddled in her seat for several seconds, refusing to believe that the evening could end like this. Tentatively she stretched out her hand to touch Gil's arm. 'Gil, please . . .'

He jerked away, as though her touch revolted him. 'I told you before, I don't want to hear. Now get out.'

'But you don't understand. I love you,' she whispered desperately, the pain of Gil's rejection stronger than her pride.

'Love?' he jeered. 'You don't know the meaning of the word. Did you *love* your young Lothario too? Do you think that's all there is to it? A quick tumble in the grass? That's not love, that's lust, and you haven't begun to learn the difference.'

Horribly humiliated, Olivia almost vaulted out of the door in her rush to get away from him. How could she ever face him again? At that moment she hated herself but, perversely, she hated Gil more. He had thrown her love back in her face and trampled her dreams into dust, and she could never forgive him for it.

The very next day, Gil returned to America, and although she had heard of him intermittently via Vivien during the intervening years they had never seen each other again. Until today.

The bath water had gone cold, Olivia realised with a shiver. Standing up and reaching for a towel, she was dismayed to discover that her cheeks felt damp, as if she'd been crying. Nonsense, she told herself firmly, it's steam. But she couldn't easily shrug off the gnawing pain in the pit of her stomach.

CHAPTER THREE

OLIVIA listened to the buzz of noisy chatter coming from around the large oval table in the agency's main conference room and wished she could share the general enthusiasm.

Gil's appointment had prompted a wave of excitement and speculation among all the staff at Beaufort's but the senior personnel were particularly eager to meet their new managing director. He was already known to most of them, by name if not in person, and all wanted to hear of his plans for Beaufort's and assess how much their own positions would be affected by his arrival.

None of them could possibly be affected as much as her, Olivia thought gloomily. None of them was likely to have his or her existing post snatched from him and set to work in an unknown job, for a person whom he disliked intensely.

Her pessimistic mood wasn't helped by the fact that she'd slept badly the night before. Far from exorcising Gil, reviving memories of that summer only seemed to have entrenched him more deeply in her thoughts. She'd tossed and turned until the early hours of the morning, haunted by his image, her body hot and restless as it remembered the feel of his hands on her.

'He's related to you, isn't he?' Carol Dailey, seated on Olivia's right, asked suddenly, jolting her out of her reverie.

'What? Oh—er—yes. Distantly.'

'What's he like?' Carol prompted. 'I've been told he's very sexy.'

Olivia gulped. 'He's—um——' She paused, wondering how on earth to respond to that. What could she say about Gil which wouldn't immediately reveal her own antagonism towards him? Proclaiming her dislike for her new boss to all and sundry wouldn't be a very diplomatic start to their working relationship, after all. 'We—er—we haven't met for a long time. I haven't seen him in years,' she side-stepped the question.

Carol gave her a speculative look. 'How intriguing! Why not? A family feud?'

'No...nothing like that,' Olivia hastened to quell her conjectures. Carol was a renowned gossip and loved nothing more than a bit of scandal to get her teeth into. 'With Gil working in America and me here, our paths never crossed, that's all.'

'He's not married, is he?'

'No.'

'What about serious girlfriends?'

Olivia decided that she didn't like the direction this conversation was taking. 'I really have no idea.'

Carol giggled. 'It's OK. I'm just checking out the opposition. Our new managing director's quite a catch, you know.'

Olivia did know but she didn't like the disagreeable thoughts that Carol's questions had produced. *Did* Gil have a girlfriend in New York? What a ridiculously coy term. Gil wouldn't have girlfriends, he would have lovers. And why should it matter to her if he did?

There was a flurry of activity in the doorway and Carol gave a low, appreciative whistle under her breath as Gil entered. 'So, the rumours weren't exaggerated after all. He *is* very sexy,' she murmured.

Gil was more formally dressed than yesterday but looked every bit as attractive, Olivia noted reluctantly. A charcoal-grey suit emphasised his dark good looks, reinforcing rather than disguising the leanly muscled physique beneath. It wasn't difficult to see what had prompted Carol's comment and Olivia guessed it would be a view shared by most of the other female staff, regardless of age or status. Why did that thought produce a sensation far too closely akin to jealousy for her liking?

He took his seat at the head of the table and silence fell on the assembled group as he introduced himself. 'Good morning. My name is Gil and I'm the new managing director of Beaufort's.'

An hour later, Olivia sensed that everyone was duly impressed by what they had seen and heard. Justifiably so.

Gil was an excellent communicator. With swift precision, he had set out his plans for the agency, offering reassurances that there would be no drastic changes in the short term but pointing out areas for future development and expansion.

Initial wariness gave way to enthusiasm as Gil's own commitment to Beaufort's became evident.

He invited questions and dealt with each point raised calmly and confidently, neither ducking out on difficult answers nor allowing himself to be forced into giving more information than he was prepared to on other, less clear-cut issues.

As a major shareholder, Olivia knew she should have been reassured that Beaufort's was in good hands but, as an employee, it wasn't the agency's future which worried her most right now, it was her own. If only she could have kept on her old job, seen as little of Gil as possible, then perhaps she wouldn't have felt so dispirited. It was the knowledge that she would be expected to work alongside him, day after day, for two whole years which filled her with such dread.

His talk concluded, Gil handed out sheets detailing appointments he had made in order to talk to each senior member of staff individually. With a sinking heart, Olivia noted that her name appeared at the very top of the list and her meeting with him was the first one scheduled for the afternoon. Evidently he didn't intend to waste any time before instructing her in her new duties.

Nearly three hours later, she faced Gil across his desk. She'd spent the lunch-hour preparing herself, mentally and physically. She looked fine, she knew that. The very simplicity of her navy wool suit bespoke its quality. If only her nerves could as easily be cut and trimmed to suit the occasion. She wondered if he could see the slight tremor of her fingers.

If he did, he evidently didn't feel any shred of sympathy. 'Have you dealt with the transfer of your accounts yet?' he demanded without preamble.

Good lord! Did the man think she worked all night as well as all day? 'It'll take some time to hand them over. A week at least. I can't just pass them on without some discussion with the new executives who are going to deal with them,' she protested.

There was a brief pause as Gil's deep brown eyes narrowed on hers in a long, assessing look. 'OK, I accept the hand-over may take a little while to accomplish but I don't want you using that as an excuse to delay starting work as my assistant.'

'I'm not——'

'No? Don't let's play games, Olivia. You admitted yesterday that you don't like that condition in your grandmother's will, you don't like my being the new managing director, and you don't like the fact that you've got to work for me.'

He'd summed up her views pretty well, Olivia acknowledged. 'Would you like it if you were in my position?' she demanded.

'No, I wouldn't.'

His calm admission took some of the wind out of her sails. She frowned. 'Well, then?'

'But if it couldn't be altered ... and this can't ... I'd accept it and make the best of it.'

Would he? Olivia wondered. Gil wasn't the sort of man who bowed to the dictates of others. He stated his own terms, not the other way round.

She was willing to bet he would fight that condition every step of the way, yet he seemed to expect her to meekly comply with it. 'That's easier said than done,' she said curtly.

He stood upright and moved round the desk to face her, edging a hip on to the edge. 'Yes, it is,' he agreed, 'but I've been looking through your personnel file——' He indicated the paperwork on his desk. 'And, according to the reports, you're good at your job. Very good.'

'Thank you,' Olivia said stiffly, taken aback by the unexpected tribute and not liking the reaction his closer proximity had provoked. The tiny hairs on her skin seemed to have gone on danger alert. She wasn't used to responding like this to men, neither at work nor socially. It made her feel uncomfortable and nervous. She didn't feel in control, of herself or the situation.

'Don't thank me, thank your previous department heads. That's their opinion of your abilities, not mine,' Gil said drily. 'I haven't had an opportunity to assess your work yet but I'm willing to keep an open mind on the subject. Perhaps you should try doing the same about working for me.'

Olivia stared at him, momentarily lost for words. What on earth had made her think he was actually being pleasant? The man was infuriating! He made her feel like a skittle—set upright only to be bowled over by him yet again.

'You still haven't given me any details of what my job will be as your assistant,' she said through gritted teeth.

Gil stood up again and moved to the window, looking out. His stance had all the lithe grace of a lean black panther as he slid his hands deep into his trouser pockets. 'You heard what I said at the meeting this morning. Beaufort's has a respectable list of blue-chip accounts in this country but it needs to attract international clients if it's going to expand. Several of my clients from Rossaro Advertising are planning to introduce media campaigns in Britain. Beaufort's can win those contracts but only if, and I repeat *if*, we can convince them the agency is capable of dealing with the sort of large-scale coverage they're looking for.'

'And can we offer that kind of extensive coverage?'

'I think so. If it's properly planned and executed. That's where you'll come in. As my assistant you'll be expected to take a share of the responsibility for the presentations we'll be submitting to prospective clients.'

Gil's gaze shifted from the window to her. 'It will be more demanding than the work you've been used to but I think you'll enjoy it—if you don't let your personal feelings come between you and the job, that is.'

Olivia felt herself bristling. Gil might be able to separate his professional and personal life into two distinct compartments without difficulty, but she doubted she could manage it so easily. Even now, her thoughts were horribly tangled.

She still had some reservations about his proposals for Beaufort's but, properly handled, she could see how they would benefit the agency.

Professionally her quick brain had already sensed the opportunities this new job presented and was eager to respond to those challenges, but on a personal level she dreaded having to work so closely to Gil. She couldn't even be in the same room as him without feeling as if she was in some kind of danger.

'I'll do my best,' she said stiffly.

'Make sure you do,' Gil replied. 'I don't believe in giving second chances.'

Professionally or personally, Olivia thought with a wave of foreboding.

He glanced at his watch, indicating that their interview was at an end. 'I'm willing to give you a week to get those transfers arranged. After that you'll be working here.' He indicated the adjoining office.

Olivia shivered as she stood up to go. Why did it feel as if she'd just received a threat?

As soon as she got back to her apartment, Olivia set about preparing the treat she had promised herself throughout the bitterly cold journey home. It wasn't much of a treat as treats went, but it was exactly the sort of self-cosseting she needed after one of the hardest weeks she'd ever known. Somehow she had managed to get all her accounts transferred, but only by working late every evening. Tonight she'd been determined to get away on time and pamper herself a little before the ordeal of facing Gil first thing in the morning. The prospect filled her with panic and she deliberately pushed the unpleasant thought aside. Time enough to worry about that tomorrow.

A quick shower and change of clothes, then supper on a tray while she watched an old Western on TV. It would fill the evening and hopefully shut out all thoughts of what awaited her the next day. She rummaged through the freezer for a home-made quiche and set it to heat in the oven.

She'd just stepped out of the shower, dripping wet, when the buzzer on the intercom sounded. Mildly irritated, Olivia slipped a towel round herself before going through to the hallway to flick the switch. 'Who is it?'

'It's me.'

Only one person could say that with the supremely arrogant knowledge that she would recognise his voice straight away. Instinctively Olivia pulled the towel more tightly round her. What on earth was Gil doing at her apartment? 'What do you want?'

'To talk to you.'

'Yes?'

An impatient sigh sounded. 'Not via an intercom system.'

'You've just got me out of the shower,' she protested.

'So?'

'I'm standing here without a stitch of——' Just in time she clamped her mouth shut on the incriminating description.

'Stark naked, huh? Well, don't worry about it on my account.'

His amusement filtered through the speaker and Olivia felt herself blushing all over. Why had she said that? Why hadn't she just made up some excuse about it being inconvenient? 'I'll let you in when I get dressed,' she said tersely.

'For God's sake, Olivia. It's freezing cold out here.'

'Good!' she murmured under her breath and flicked the switch off with a satisfied click.

Unhurriedly she made her way through to the bedroom. She wouldn't rush. Let him freeze. With a bit of luck, he might give up and go away altogether. She pulled back the heavy door of the wall-length wardrobe and surveyed the contents. Left to her own devices, she would simply have selected a silk nightdress and matching robe but with the threat of Gil's arrival to consider she had to change her mind. She couldn't greet him in a nightie!

In the end, she decided on a deliberately asexual outfit, pulling out a comfortably baggy tracksuit and tossing it onto the bed. Its pink and emerald stripes flattered her colouring but no one could accuse her of wearing it to appear seductive.

She'd pulled her hair up into a loose topknot before getting into the shower and she reached up with one hand to release it now. For some reason her hair proved less obliging than usual, or perhaps she wasn't imagining the slight tremor in her fingers, and Olivia was obliged to drop the towel she'd been holding round herself in order to deal with it.

Once her hair was loose about her shoulders, Olivia didn't bother to pick the towel up again. The apartment was warm and she wasn't self-conscious about her own nakedness, at least not when she was alone. She'd always been slender in build and the daily exercise regime she'd devised kept her body firmly toned; catching sight of herself in the mirror held no horrors for her.

It wasn't her own reflection which made her halt and gasp in horror now. She could scarcely believe what she was seeing. What the hell was Gil doing, standing negligently in the open doorway of her bedroom?

Shocked, she swung round to face him, a furious riposte already forming on her lips. Yet for some reason the explosion never came. Gil's expression halted it. He made no attempt to conceal the unequivocal sexual appreciation in his gaze, but was she mistaken in sensing more to his look than sexual appraisal, more to the hunger expressed there than mere fulfilment of appetite?

The hiatus could only have been momentary for within seconds Gil's expression changed, making Olivia doubt the accuracy of her own confused observations. When his features assumed that lazily amused aspect which always infuriated her, she berated her own folly in ever suspecting some deeper expression of longing behind the mockery. Blushing crimson, she belatedly grabbed the discarded towel from the floor and wrapped it round herself.

'How did you get in?' she demanded.

'One of the other residents took pity on me and opened the door,' he informed her.

'Did they? Who was it? No one is supposed to do that. It's against the association rules. And how dare you march into my apartment without knocking?' Olivia babbled wildly.

'Your door was unlocked so I let myself in.' Gil's casual explanation of his appearance suggested that he'd surprised her in the act of nothing more embarrassing than tying up a shoelace. His very nonchalance made her more enraged than ever. Damn the man! He could at least apologise for this... this invasion of her privacy.

'You could have knocked. How dare you sneak in like this?'

Gil shrugged. 'I did knock but evidently you didn't hear. There's no need for such hysterics, Olivia. You're hardly the first woman I've seen naked.'

'Maybe not, but you're...' Olivia bit down hard on the admission, belatedly realising its implications. Gil no doubt thought she'd notched up numerous lovers by now. He wasn't to know that no man had ever seen her without her clothes.

'I'm what?' One dark brow lifted curiously.

'You're not my lover,' she flung at him recklessly. 'I'm choosy about whom I invite into my bedroom and I don't expect to find intruders prying on me in the privacy of my own home.'

Gil leaned an elbow against the door-frame and raked a hand through the thick blackness of his hair in a weary gesture. 'It was an accident,

Olivia. I let myself in and before I could locate you I saw this door was open. I didn't realise it was your bedroom. If you feel your privacy has been violated, I'm sorry.'

The apology was so unexpected that Olivia found herself staring at Gil in stunned silence. She knew she should accept it at face value, and coming from anyone else she probably would have done, but the turbulent reaction she'd experienced on seeing his eyes on her had shattered all her usual reasonableness. Her shock needed an outlet. She wanted to strike out and dent Gil's composure just as he had done hers.

'There's a name for men like you.'

Gil's gaze darkened warningly. 'And there's a name for women like you Olivia, only until now I've been too polite to use it. I find it hard to believe that a woman of your sexual experience can be so outraged over such an incident. I could see more female flesh exposed by visiting a Mediterranean beach. Or do you consider your body so unique that it differs from the rest of the female sex? I assure you it doesn't.'

Olivia felt herself almost shaking with fury. 'When I want your views on the female anatomy, I'll ask for them. No doubt you're an expert on the subject.'

Gil turned unhurriedly towards the doorway, the hard line of his mouth quirking as he delivered his parting shot. 'I prefer to think of myself as a connoisseur.'

As the door closed, Olivia felt like hurling something sharp and painful at Gil's departing back. She sat down weakly on the edge of her bed and stared at her reflection in the mirror, noting her flushed cheeks and the rapid rise and fall of her breasts. She tried to tell herself that her rumpled appearance was due to a fully justified anger at encountering Gil in such humiliating circumstances, but her conscience balked against the uneasy insistence. For a short time at least, she knew that her response had waited on his. What had she thought she'd seen in his eyes in those first few seconds? Warmth? Desire? Passion? And if she'd been right, would her subsequent reaction have been different?

When she entered the lounge a few minutes later, she noted that Gil had already discarded his suit jacket, helped himself to a drink and was now browsing through the *Financial Times*, looking for all the world like a relaxed cat making itself at home. It seemed strange to find him here, like this, in her domain. He should have looked odd, out of place, yet somehow he didn't. He looked as if he belonged. For a moment, Olivia found the awareness strangely comforting and then rapidly quashed the sensation. It was far too dangerous.

'Do make yourself at home,' she invited.

'I already have,' Gil assured her, ignoring her sarcasm.

Olivia went to the drinks cabinet to mix herself a drink. Even in a loose tracksuit, she felt horribly self-conscious, vividly remembering the expression in Gil's eyes as they had viewed her naked body.

His gaze took in her casual outfit. 'You're not going out tonight?'

'No.'

'No date?'

What the hell had it got to do with him anyway? 'Not tonight,' she said tightly, hoping to imply it was a change rather than the norm. 'What did you want to see me about anyway?' She wanted to get this meeting over and done with as quickly as possible and send Gil on his way.

He took a swig of his drink. 'I tried to see you before you left work this evening but when I got through to your office you'd already left.'

'I hope you're not trying to make out I'm some sort of clock-watcher,' Olivia leapt hotly to her own defence. 'I've worked late every evening this week. Tonight was the first one when I got away on time.'

'Relax, Olivia. It was a statement of fact. Not an accusation.'

His soothing tone mollified Olivia a little and she took a deep, restraining breath. 'Well, then?'

'I wanted to let you know about a meeting I've arranged for nine-thirty tomorrow morning. It's with some representatives of one of the Japanese car companies. We're only discussing ideas at this stage but I'd like you to be there.'

Somewhat appeased, she nodded. 'All right.'

'It's important, so don't be late.'

Olivia bridled. 'I was brought up to consider punctuality——'

She didn't get any further as Gil suddenly sniffed the air appreciatively and demanded, 'Mmm, that smells good. What is it?'

'Oh, goodness! The quiche!' Olivia had completely forgotten about the supper she'd put in the oven earlier. In a sudden flurry of activity, she leapt up from her chair and raced through to the kitchen.

In fact the quiche was cooked to perfection, its surface an appetising golden-brown. And it smelled delicious.

'Are you expecting someone or is that all for you?'

Olivia hadn't realised that Gil had followed her through to the kitchen. That fact and the unexpected question took her by surprise. She swung round to face him, oven-gloves still in her hands, cheeks flushed from the hot cooker. 'No...I...that is...'

'You couldn't possibly eat all that yourself.'

There was a teasing note to his voice which caught her off guard. It reminded her so much of the way he'd used to speak to her five years ago. Her eyes swept over his dark features, as if trying to relocate something of the man she'd once known. She saw the shadows beneath his eyes and the evidence of weariness in their depths, noted the jawline stubble beginning to emerge.

He's had a hard day too, she thought, on a sudden rush of tenderness. 'Would you like to share it with me?' The spontaneous question was uttered almost before Olivia realised what she was saying, prompted wholly by feelings, not reasons. In fact she could have come up with a hundred reasons against issuing such an invitation.

In an instant, she felt horribly vulnerable, as if she'd just dropped her guard against the enemy.

Without even waiting for Gil's reply, she turned away from him and busied herself getting plates, and knives and forks, hoping he would not notice the tremor in her hands as she set them out on the work surface. With some difficulty, she cut the quiche into slices and slid one on to each plate.

They carried them back through to the lounge and each ate in silence for several minutes. Olivia was too appalled at what she had done to derive any pleasure from the food. It might as well have been cardboard in her mouth. Only half an hour before she had been spitting daggers at Gil after finding him in her bedroom and now she was sharing a meal with him as if that scene had never taken place. Was she mad? Her only hope of survival lay in keeping him at as great a distance as possible. She might as well have invited a man-eating tiger into her home.

Gil, however, seemed to have no such constraints on his appetite and finished the quiche while Olivia was still pushing hers round her plate. She felt like an over-wound spring, ready to leap at any moment, and couldn't bear to try to eat with Gil lounging back in his chair, watching her.

'I'll...I'll make us some coffee.' She jumped up from her chair and hurried through to the kitchen.

Desperately putting off the moment when she must face him again, Olivia took as long as possible over preparing the coffee. When she finally carried the tray back into the lounge, she was horrified to discover him sleeping in the chair.

She set the tray down on the table and stared at him for several minutes, wondering what on earth she should do. She wasn't used to finding sleeping men in her home, especially not men like Gil. Even at rest there was a potent energy about him which paradoxically both frightened and fascinated her. A fierce desire strained inside her, making her want to kneel down beside him and run her fingers through the thick blackness of his hair, to trace the stubble-roughened angle of his cheek, and on down to brush against the shadow of darkly curling chest hair just visible below the open neck of his shirt.

Why... why did it have to be Gil who made her feel like this? In the last five years she had dated a number of men yet none had ever affected her in this way. By what cruel trick did her body respond so wilfully to him alone?

She hardly dared touch him yet she couldn't simply leave him either. He looked exhausted enough to sleep right through the night.

She shook his shoulder, trying not to be aware of how hard the lean muscles felt beneath her fingers. 'Gil ... Gil, wake up.'

After what seemed an age, Gil eventually opened his eyes and yawned. 'Did I fall asleep?' he murmured.

Olivia nodded.

He stretched. 'You should just have left me. I wouldn't have stirred till morning.'

'That's what I was afraid of,' Olivia retorted drily.

'Why, did you have other plans for this evening?' Gil demanded, some of the languor leaving his expression.

As the full implication of the question filtered through, Olivia drew away from him stiffly. 'No, I did not,' she denied. 'But I . . . I couldn't have let you spend the night here.'

Gil gave a husky laugh. 'Why not? I can assure you, you would have been quite safe. You must know by now that sheer physical exhaustion is as effective as any chaperon.'

Olivia could hardly believe she was having this conversation with him. It was positively indecent. A crimson stain suffused her cheeks. 'That's . . . that's not the point,' she spluttered. 'I . . . I don't want my neighbours thinking you've spent the night here.'

'I wondered about the single bed. Presumably it discourages your lovers from staying over,' Gil mused with apparent indifference, though his eyes watched her steadily.

Olivia found herself unable to hold his gaze. She couldn't carry on this conversation about single beds and lovers. It was all too much. Much too much. 'I think you'd better go,' she said tautly.

Just then the buzzer sounded. Olivia glanced down at her watch. Who on earth could be calling at this time? she wondered as she went to the door.

'Hi, Olivia. I've brought that suitcase over that you promised to store for me. Sorry to call so late but I'm planning to leave very early in the morning.'

'That's—er—all right, Nick. Come in,' Olivia invited, holding the door open and trying to collect her fragmented thoughts together.

She recalled Nick asking her about the suitcase earlier in the week. He'd just sold a neighbouring apartment but his new home wasn't ready to move into and he was distributing various possessions temporarily among friends.

'You've got a visitor?' Gil materialised beside her, pulling on his suit jacket. There was a hard edge to his voice as he glanced down at the suitcase.

'Yes.' Olivia didn't see why she should offer him explanations. Her visitor was none of his business.

Nick swung the case further into the hallway and deposited it on the floor with a resounding thud. His cheerful grin slipped away in the face of Gil's narrowed look of displeasure.

'I hope I'm not disturbing anything,' he said awkwardly, looking uncertainly from Olivia to Gil and then back again.

'No——' Olivia began but Gil beat her to it.

'No, Olivia and I were just finished. She's all yours.'

And then, quite unexpectedly, Gil's arm slid round Olivia's waist, pulling her to him, and he kissed her hard on the lips.

Taken totally by surprise, Olivia could only sway weakly against him, close enough to hear him whisper throatily in her ear, 'See what your lover makes of that.'

Seconds later he was gone and Olivia was left with only the imprint of his body against hers and a mouth which felt bruised by his rough possession of it. She stared dazedly after him, not stirring until Nick enquired tentatively, 'Are you all right?'

She nodded weakly. 'Yes... Yes, I'm all right,' knowing perfectly well that she was uttering a lie. She felt anything but all right. She felt as if her whole world had just been turned upside-down.

A few minutes later Nick went too, leaving Olivia alone. She went straight to bed, desperate for the oblivion of sleep but finding her thoughts more tormented than ever. Her mind was racked with images of Gil and her body was tormented by the memory of his lean hardness as he'd pulled her against him. Why hadn't she resisted him then? Pulled away from him...slapped him even? Self-respect alone demanded that she should have done far more than simply curve submissively against him as she had.

CHAPTER FOUR

OLIVIA awoke groggily to stare at her alarm clock in dismay. Eleven o'clock! It couldn't be! She rubbed her eyes and stared at the gilt-edged face again. Oh, no! Somehow she had managed to sleep through the alarm's raucous seven o'clock peal. Now she was late for work...and much too late for Gil's meeting.

She couldn't remember the last time she'd slept in until mid-morning. She should never have taken those sleeping-pills. After tossing and turning for nearly three hours she'd finally given in and taken a couple of the tablets her doctor had prescribed after Vivien's death. Until now she had managed without them, but last night Gil's disturbing image and memories of his kiss had haunted her, making natural sleep impossible.

In one swift movement she swung back the covers and sat upright, then put a hand to her temple and groaned. The doctor had said that the tablets were mild but Olivia was unused to medication of any sort; she felt as if her head wasn't properly fixed to her shoulders. She knew she should hurry to get into work but doubted she was safe to drive feeling like this. Besides, there wasn't much point in rushing. Gil's meeting must be over by now. She felt terrible about missing it but there wasn't much she could do

about it now. It would be more sensible to get a
strong black cup of coffee inside her and then
face the music. Music? That was a joke. More
like a thunder roll!

Suddenly a furious banging sounded on the
door.

Olivia stayed still for a moment, her heart
thumping as she was gripped by real fear. Then
she stumbled out of bed and pulled a robe on
over her nightie as she hurried through to the entrance hall.

The banging sounded again, even louder than
before if that was possible.

'Who is it?' she asked, her heart sinking. She
already knew the answer. The thunder roll had
begun.

'Olivia, open this door.'

'No,' she said, with as much force as her dazed
senses could muster.

'If you don't open this door right now, I'm
going to break it down.'

Olivia stared at the wooden panelling in dis-
belief. He didn't sound as if he was joking.

'I . . . I don't feel very well.' She doubted that
an appeal to his sympathy would have much
effect on Gil in this bullish mood but it was worth
a try.

'For the last time, Olivia . . .'

As visions of Gil putting his shoulder to the
door filled her mind, Olivia conceded defeat. She
was in no fit state to argue. With trembling
fingers, she released the catch.

It was flung open roughly from the other side.
'Where the hell were you this morning?' he de-

manded immediately, slamming the door shut behind. 'I thought you understood me when I told you I wanted you at that meeting.'

Olivia could only stare at him dumbly, her mind too thick and woolly to make any intelligent response to the blistering outburst.

His gaze swept downwards. 'My God! You're not even dressed.'

Defensively Olivia pulled the flimsy robe more tightly round her. 'I...I overslept,' she mumbled by way of explanation.

'You overslept?' Gil sounded more furious than ever. 'No need to ask why. Did you get *any* sleep last night?'

'Well, no...hardly——'

Olivia started to explain but Gil cut off her words with whiplash anger. 'Spare me the details. I couldn't give a damn what you and your lover get up to. But I do mind when your night-time activities leave you so exhausted that you can't get to work in the morning.'

Lover...night-time activities? Olivia's eyes were two stunned pools of deep sea-green as she tried to absorb what he was saying.

'Don't give me that moonstruck look as if you don't know what I'm talking about,' Gil raged at her. 'Dispatching your lovers in the early hours of the morning may preserve your reputation but it isn't doing much for your time-keeping. Don't you think a double bed would be more honest and more practical, in every sense?'

Olivia went a deep shade of scarlet, fully alert at last. 'How dare you speak to me like this? You have no right——'

'I have every right when what you do in your spare time interferes with your work.'

'It doesn't ...'

'No?' Gil's dark eyes glittered. 'I distinctly told you to be at that meeting this morning, though...' his gaze raked insolently over her ' ... I have to admit you would hardly have been an asset. Have you looked at yourself in the mirror yet?'

'I beg your pardon?'

'You look wiped out...exhausted,' Gil said bluntly. 'You're a lousy advertisement for the agency. You couldn't even sell yourself, let alone a product.'

Olivia stared at him as hurt and anger at the deliberate insult combined together in one explosive package.

She dared not even trust herself to speak. Turning on her heel, she went to move away from Gil but his hand clamped on her shoulder, twisting her back to face him.

Perhaps if she hadn't struggled he would have let her go, but his restraining grip was the last straw. Her hands flailed wildly, not caring where they landed. There was a few seconds' struggle before Gil grabbed both her wrists and pushed her back against the wall, holding her still.

Olivia's breath came in harsh gasps and the blood pounded in her ears as she looked up into his face, noting the darkened flush on his cheekbones.

For an interminable length of time, they stared at each other and then abruptly Gil's expression changed. He was still angry, Olivia knew that, but now there was something else too. She searched his face, trying to decipher his thoughts, but could see only the velvety blackness of his pupils as they focused on her mouth.

For a few seconds, her heart seemed to stop beating and then, as Gil's lips covered hers, it leapt in response.

Seconds...minutes passed—Olivia had no idea how long. All she knew was the fierce longing which Gil's kiss had released and which swept through her whole being.

His hands caressed her, drawing her to him and making her come alive in a way she had experienced only once before. Not since she was eighteen, and in Gil's arms, had her body felt so totally responsive.

Instinctively she arched against him, seeking to assuage the need which gripped her.

Suddenly, though, his mouth left hers and his hands dropped. When Olivia opened her eyes it was to find him staring down at her, an odd, almost disbelieving look on his face.

With an inward groan, she shut her eyes, desperately wishing the last few moments undone, and when she opened them again that expression was gone.

In its place was a steely gaze which made him seem more distant and remote than ever.

She choked back a sob, drawing a swift, searing taunt from Gil. 'Crying, Olivia? Is that from relief or frustration?'

The desire to slap the cool mockery from his face was instantaneous and Olivia's hand was halfway there before Gil halted it, his fingers closing on her wrists like handcuffs.

'Don't do it,' he advised softly. 'My reactions are twice as fast as yours.'

Slowly he released his grip and she rubbed her wrists conspicuously.

'I think you'd better get dressed.'

'Dressed?' Olivia felt so dazed that she could hardly comprehend what he was saying.

'Unless you're planning to go in to work in that,' he said insolently, his gaze skimming downwards.

Olivia snatched the robe to her. 'Of course not. But——'

'But what?'

'You can't expect me to work for you after this.'

'Are you offering me your resignation?'

The swift retort startled her. 'No, of course not!' she denied. If she resigned, then she would lose entitlement to all her grandmother's shares.

'Well, what are you offering?' Gil's eyes glittered suggestively.

Olivia cursed herself for blushing. 'A compromise?'

'I think you're compromised quite enough already,' Gil said drily.

'I want my old job back.'

'No.'

The unequivocal response made it clear that her suggestion wasn't open to discussion and Olivia stared at him helplessly. 'You can't really want me to work for you?'

Gil gave her a long, cold look. 'Wanting has nothing to do with it, Olivia. I'm prepared to put professional needs above personal inclinations, that's all. I suggest you try doing the same and then perhaps we won't have a repeat of this performance.'

With that, he reached for the door-handle and yanked it open. 'I expect you in your office in one hour. Don't be late.'

Olivia listened to his footsteps receding down the corridor and then sank to the floor, her body gripped by shuddering sobs. She had never been so humiliated in her life before. Except once, and then by the same man.

She hated him! Hated him! Yet even as she uttered the savage words she knew they were lies. If she hated him, she could never have let him touch her as he had, could never have responded to his touch as she had. The dull, throbbing ache inside her told her that much at least.

Olivia stretched, catlike, easing muscles grown cramped from sitting in front of a word processor for most of the afternoon and evening. She felt tired, but satisfied. The report was finally finished and would be on Gil's desk first thing in the morning.

It told him everything he needed to know about the soft drinks campaign Beaufort's was planning for one of the big American manufacturers, from target groups to proposed magazine and television slots for the adverts themselves. Despite her initial resistance to embarking on the project, Olivia had soon found it a fascinating and absorbing exercise.

She hoped Gil would be pleased with it. For reasons she couldn't fully explain, his approval was important to her.

She had been apprehensive—more than apprehensive—terrified of facing him after that morning just over two weeks ago when he'd come round to her apartment, but somehow she had steeled herself to go into work, knowing that if she didn't do it then she would lose her nerve. She hadn't known what reception to expect from Gil and had been almost as wary of the icy politeness he had greeted her with as she had been of his hot fury earlier.

But gradually reserve had given way to a grudging respect. It wasn't difficult to see what made Gil so successful in the advertising world; he had a brilliant mind, combining a businessman's precision with an artist's creative flair, and Olivia had to confess to an increasing admiration of his abilities.

The shrill jangle of the telephone in Gil's neighbouring office made her jump and she hurried to answer it, dithering for a moment between the two phones on his desk, before realising that it was the private line ringing.

'Yes? Can I help you? This is the managing director's office.'

'I know it's the managing director's office,' a female voice, with a husky American accent, drawled. 'I want to speak to Gil.' The slight emphasis on the last word subtly implied a relationship which had long since dispensed with the formality of titles.

Olivia bristled, instantly disliking both the familiarity and the bored arrogance in the tone.

'I'm afraid he's already gone home,' she said curtly.

'Already?' The woman sounded sceptical.

'It is after eight o'clock here,' Olivia pointed out.

'That's nothing to Gil. Here he was often at his desk till midnight. God! The hours we spent in that office.'

'We?' The rejoinder was a little too quick, a little too sharp, and Olivia could have bitten her tongue off as soon as it was uttered, fully aware of its revelations.

A throaty laugh gurgled down the phone. 'All in the interests of duty, I assure you. I'm Susannah Whitlow. I used to be Gil's PA at Rossaro Advertising.'

Duty my eye, Olivia thought crossly. It's not her devotion to duty she's trying to impress on me, it's her familiarity with Gil. Was familiarity strong enough? Should that be intimacy?

'Who are you?'

'I'm Olivia Beaufort.'

The brief silence which followed suddenly seemed charged with tension and Olivia could almost feel the other woman's dislike crackling down the line. When she spoke again all traces of husky humour had gone and there was a sharp edge to her voice.

'Ah! The little cousin! The one who's now working for Gil.'

Who had told her that? Olivia wondered. Gil himself?

'That's right.'

'And are you enjoying being his *personal* assistant?'

The slight emphasis on that one word implied an involvement which went far beyond the office. Just how involved had Susannah and Gil been when she was his PA? Olivia wondered, hating the unpleasant sensation the question provoked.

'The work is fascinating,' she said coolly, refusing to allow herself to be goaded into a more revealing response.

'And Gil's a fascinating man. Wouldn't you agree?'

'As a boss, he certainly commands respect.'

Susannah gave a small laugh. 'Boss? Respect? Come now, aren't those terms rather formal? Surely you know Gil a little better than that by now?'

The woman was obviously jealous and Olivia guessed she was fishing to try and discover whether there was any involvement between her and Gil outside working hours.

It was so far from the truth that Olivia would have laughed if she hadn't found Susannah's probing questions so offensive.

'Is there any message you would like me to give him?' she asked at last, pointedly ignoring the last remark.

There was a small silence as Susannah absorbed the rebuff and Olivia wondered what she was thinking.

'No,' she said abruptly. 'I would prefer to talk to him personally. This isn't really a business call, you see.'

Olivia did see, with crystal clarity. Gil and this woman had been lovers and the mere matter of an ocean between them wasn't going to end the affair, at least not as far as she was concerned.

'In that case I suggest you contact him on his home number,' she said shortly and settled the receiver back in its cradle with a shaky clatter.

The call had spoiled her earlier mood of satisfaction at getting the report finished. Her insides were churning and she felt tense and edgy... but not jealous, she told herself sternly. The fact that Susannah had been—maybe still was—Gil's lover meant nothing to her. Why should it?

'Who was that?'

Olivia swung round to find Gil standing in the doorway. She thought he'd gone home long ago. His unexpected appearance made her gaze at him in startled surprise. Divested of his jacket and tie, and with the top buttons of his shirt undone, he looked different, much less formal than usual and infinitely more disturbing.

'It... it was Susannah Whitlow.'

'Susannah Whitlow?' Gil frowned. 'What did she want?'

'I don't know. She wouldn't leave a message. She wanted to speak to you personally.'

She tried to detect Gil's reaction to that piece of information but his expression was unreadable, giving no clue to his feelings.

Perhaps he was waiting for her to go so that he could return Susannah's call in privacy. She moved towards the doorway to return to her own office but his hand on her shoulder halted her.

Instantly she recoiled as though he'd hurt her, such was the violence of her reaction to his touch.

His eyes narrowed and his hands dropped swiftly, sliding deep into the pockets of his trousers. 'Did she upset you in some way?' he demanded abruptly.

Shaken by the phone call and perturbed by her reaction to Gil, Olivia was on the defensive. 'Of course not! Why should she upset me?' Then, because she didn't want to hear any answer he might give to that, 'I...I really must be going. I was just about to leave when your phone rang,' Olivia murmured, easing herself carefully past him and going through to her own office. To her dismay he followed her.

'Why were you here so late?' he asked.

Olivia glanced down at the portfolio on her desk. 'I...I've been working on the project. It's all done...finished.'

Gil inclined his head slightly. 'I'm impressed. I thought it would take you at least another couple of weeks to complete. Well done.'

A blush of pleasure stained Olivia's cheeks and she wondered why praise from Gil should be so ridiculously pleasing.

Footsteps sounded in the corridor and one of the night porters paused outside the office door. 'Sorry, I thought everyone had gone,' he apologised for the interruption.

'We're just on our way,' Gil told him.

Olivia hurriedly grabbed her briefcase and began to pull on her coat, tugging the belt tight at her waist.

In the lift, Gil automatically pressed the button to take them both down to the basement and the underground car park.

'I'll get out at the ground floor. My car wouldn't start this morning so I caught a taxi to work,' Olivia explained hurriedly.

The lift was reasonably spacious but, enclosed in it with Gil, she felt almost claustrophobic. He filled her senses, overwhelming them until breathing itself became an effort. He hadn't bothered to replace his tie and at the open V of his shirt she glimpsed a blur of darkly curling chest hairs and her nostrils filled with a potent male scent.

It wasn't fair that he should affect her like this . . . so effortlessly.

'You're not planning to walk home, are you?'

Olivia shook her head. 'No, I'll call a taxi from the security office.'

'No need. I'll give you a lift.'

'No . . . no. I can easily call a taxi,' she protested.

'Don't be ridiculous, Olivia. My apartment isn't far from yours so it's not taking me out of my way to drop you off. I'm only offering to give you a lift, you know, not proposing,' Gil said drily.

Put like that, he made her refusal sound petty and ungracious, as if she was making mountains out of molehills, and Olivia regarded him in mute vexation as she clamped her mouth firmly shut on any further objections.

The car journey only prolonged her ordeal, as far as Olivia was concerned. If she'd been aware of Gil in the lift, she was acutely conscious of him in the much smaller confines of the car. A kind of prickly heat sensitised her limbs, as if she'd just come into contact with an allergic substance, and she grasped her briefcase to her like a defensive shield.

Apart from a few perfunctory exchanges, the journey was silent and Olivia spent most of the time gazing out of the window. Since the streets were quiet now, it didn't take long and she gave a sigh of relief as they turned into her road. Relief which quickly turned to dismay as she caught sight of Nick's car outside her apartment block.

'I see you have a visitor,' Gil said drily, drawing to a halt beside the pavement.

'Yes ... well, thank you for the lift,' Olivia replied swiftly, and got out, hoping he would drive straight on.

But for some reason Gil's car remained stationary and Olivia had no choice but to turn her attention to Nick and the girl with him.

'Hi, Olivia. I'm glad I managed to catch you. You remember Jennifer, don't you? We've come to pick up the suitcase. Thanks for looking after it for me... Now we've moved in to the new place, Jennifer can't wait to get started on a few housewifely duties, like ironing all those crumpled clothes. Can you, darling?' And he gave Jennifer a teasing hug.

Olivia knew that Gil could hear every word through the open window of his car. She was irritated that he had delayed his departure to eavesdrop on the conversation. He might own her body and soul at the office but her private life had nothing to do with him. She hadn't pried into the details of his relationship with Susannah Whitlow, had she?

He must now realise that Nick was not her lover at all. Perhaps she should be relieved that the foolish deception was over, but she wasn't. She wasn't relieved at all. She felt suddenly afraid, as if she'd just been stripped of her protective armour.

'Come on up to the apartment,' she invited Nick and Jennifer, leading the way. By the time she'd reached the entrance, Gil's car had disappeared.

CHAPTER FIVE

OLIVIA woke very early the following morning. She tossed and turned for some time before finally admitting that she wouldn't be able to get back to sleep again and getting up to make herself a cup of tea. But even that didn't settle the butterflies in her stomach.

What's the matter with you? she thought crossly, gripping the steaming mug tightly between her fingers.

A few months ago she'd been quite happy with her life; she had her job, her friends, and as active a social life as she wanted. She'd never suffered broken nights' sleep and when she woke in the mornings she'd known what to expect of each day. Why was everything so different now? Silly question. She already knew the answer. Gil was what made everything so different.

He had turned her life upside-down—professionally and personally. And even though she seemed to have got her working life into some sort of order her private life was more mixed up than ever. Why couldn't she get him out of her thoughts? All right, so he knew the truth about Nick. What difference did it make? Gil had probably already filed that piece of information away as of no importance. Why couldn't she do the same?

What she needed was some absorbing physical activity which would demand all her attention and focus her thoughts on a much less dangerous object than Gil Rossaro.

On impulse, she went through to the bedroom and changed into a purple tracksuit. She had an hour before she needed to get ready for work—plenty of time to go jogging. At one time she'd gone out regularly every morning but over the last few months she'd let it lapse. Now would be a good time to start again, especially with the incentive of spring mornings to look forward to.

Even at this early hour, the park was busy; there were other joggers like herself, dog-walkers, people taking the scenic route to work. But Olivia hardly noticed anyone else as soon as the steady beat of her feet on the paths caught her in its rhythm.

She knew how to pace herself, how to push her body to the point where it felt charged by the energetic pounding of her heartbeat, the point where she felt she could run and run and barely tire.

She forced herself to concentrate on her surroundings: tiny droplets of dew glistening on the grass, buds appearing on the trees, the surface of the lake lightly rippled by the breeze.

It was working. She felt invigorated and her skin glowed with the exercise. Her mind felt sharp and alert, as if it could tackle anything and anyone—even Gil Rossaro.

She was just about to turn into the tree-lined path which would take her back to the gate when she saw him coming towards her. At first she didn't believe her own eyes. It couldn't be! She must be imagining it. She was so used to him occupying her every waking thought that she was beginning to think she could see him everywhere. Her eyes strained to identify the figure in the black tracksuit.

She wasn't certain it was Gil but Olivia didn't want to hang around to find out. She veered sharply to her right, hoping that Gil, if it was him, wouldn't see her through the dense network of tree-trunks. Her breathing wasn't even any more, it was ragged as she increased her pace to put as great a distance between herself and the other jogger as possible.

Footsteps sounded behind her and then someone shouted her name. Looking back over her shoulder, she saw Gil. It was him. No doubt about it. He had almost caught up with her and she knew there was no point in trying to outrun him. She came to a reluctant standstill and tried to steady her breathing, which suddenly seemed more erratic than ever.

'Didn't you hear me calling you?' he demanded as he came to a stop beside her.

Olivia shook her head. 'Not until a moment ago,' she panted.

Gil didn't seem breathless at all. He must have been running much faster than her in order to bridge the distance between them but the effort had hardly affected him. His black hair was rumpled by the wind but that was all.

'I haven't seen you jogging here before,' Gil said.

He must come regularly, Olivia realised. She supposed that he must do some daily exercise to keep the leanly muscled physique he maintained despite long hours spent at a desk.

'I haven't been for some time. But I woke up early this morning...' Her voice trailed off. She didn't want Gil to guess the reason for her restlessness.

'Couldn't you sleep?'

The perceptive question took her by surprise. 'No...that is, yes,' she faltered. 'I just woke early, that's all.'

'Things on your mind?'

'No!' She almost startled herself with the vehemence of her own denial.

Gil gave her a narrowed look. 'I need to talk to you.'

Suddenly Olivia didn't feel in control any more. She felt very unsafe and uncertain. It didn't matter that she and Gil were standing in a public park; she felt as if they were cocooned in some private place alone, and the thought disturbed her. She wanted to get back home, where she'd feel safe. 'I'll be in work later,' she said, starting to move away from him.

'I don't want to talk about this in the office. I need to talk to you now,' he said tersely.

'I...I can't. I've got other things to do,' Olivia hedged, turning this time and starting to run in the direction of the gate.

Had she really expected Gil to leave it at that? she wondered as she heard the beat of his trainers on the path behind her. She increased her own speed but it was useless; within a few seconds, he was alongside her.

'This pace is going to hurt you a lot more than it is me,' he said with some amusement as he settled in beside her.

Olivia didn't say anything, but after only a few minutes she knew he was right. She wasn't fit enough to keep this pace up for long whereas Gil looked as if he could have maintained it all day.

By the time they reached her apartment block, her breath was coming in short, laboured gasps and she felt terrible. Her legs ached and perspiration trickled down her forehead. She knew she must look a mess; she'd gone out that morning without a scrap of make-up and with her hair caught back in a loose pony-tail. It didn't help to notice that Gil looked as relaxed and cool as if he'd been engaged in nothing more strenuous than sitting by a poolside, sipping champagne.

The knowledge ruffled her. 'Goodbye,' she said pointedly.

'I told you, I want to talk to you.'

'Well, I don't want to talk to you.' And, with that, Olivia swung round to put her key in the door and open it.

But Gil was too quick for her. As soon as the door was open, his foot was in the doorway, making it impossible to close. 'Either we talk out here or in your apartment. It makes no difference to me,' he said shortly.

Olivia glanced round. She'd already guessed what he wanted to talk to her about and she didn't relish the idea of it being broadcast in public.

'You don't leave me much choice,' she said vexedly.

'That's right,' Gil agreed, opening the door for her to precede him inside.

As soon as they reached her apartment, Olivia went through to the kitchen. She needed a drink of water. Reluctantly she offered Gil one too but he shook his head.

In his black tracksuit, he dominated the delicate white colour scheme of her kitchen. It was a large room but somehow he filled it so that it didn't matter where she stood or which way she looked—her eyes were always irresistibly drawn back to him.

'Why didn't you tell me the truth about Nick?' he demanded peremptorily.

'What about him?' Olivia deliberately pretended to misunderstand him.

'You know perfectly well what,' Gil said drily. 'He's not your lover at all.'

Olivia couldn't look at him. She had to do something else, anything. She set her glass of water down on the work surface and then reached down and began to unload the dishwasher, taking out crockery and cutlery and putting it away in cupboards and drawers.

'Is he?' Gil demanded.

Olivia briefly debated whether to lie, but what was the point? Gil knew that Nick was only a friend. 'I never said he was.'

'You let me believe it.'

'You *chose* to believe it,' she retorted hotly.

'And you *chose* not to disillusion me. Why?' Gil mimicked her own emphasis.

It was not so easy to find a swift retort to that one. She'd felt safer with an imaginary lover to act as a buffer between them; she knew that. Letting Gil think there were other men in her life had made her feel less vulnerable to him. And she didn't want him to know the truth now—that there weren't any lovers . . . there never had been. 'It . . . it wasn't any of your business,' she temporised.

'Maybe not, but what was to be gained by letting me believe it? I'm curious to know why you considered such a lie necessary.'

Panicking, Olivia picked up a handful of cutlery with trembling fingers.

'Well?' Gil repeated.

'It isn't a lie. Just because Nick isn't my lover, it doesn't mean . . .' She let the sentence trail off suggestively.

'That there aren't others,' Gil finished it for her. In an instant his arm had shot out to grab her and pull her to stand in front of him. 'Leave that,' he demanded roughly, taking the cutlery from her hand and scattering it noisily across the table. 'I know there have been others in the past. But what about now, Olivia?'

Why should it matter to him? Why did he sound as if it was so important to him? Olivia wished she knew what thoughts were going on inside his head.

Her own head felt as if a primitive drum were beating inside it. She could hardly think. All she knew was the strength of Gil's hands as they held her in front of him and the dark intensity of his gaze as he stared down at her, waiting for her answer. She swayed weakly towards him.

'Well?'

The husky demand held her spellbound and she could only gaze wide-eyed into Gil's black pupils, feeling her own dilate in their shadow. They seemed to stare at each other for one long infinite moment before he lowered his head to kiss her.

His mouth moved over hers, hungrily and urgently, opening her lips with his tongue, and sending blazing darts to dance inside her, kindling and igniting wherever they touched. Olivia felt her body grow molten and cling to Gil, as a limpet clung to hard rock for support, her fingers moving to clasp at his cotton sweatshirt and then higher to the rugged curves of his shoulders. He both drained and filled her at the same time, he knocked her world upside-down, yet he was her world and nothing...no one...else mattered. This was her worst nightmare, her wildest dream, come true.

The hands which had gripped her forearms moved lower to cup the rounded curves of her buttocks and pull her against him. Olivia shifted her stance willingly, curving her body to Gil's, drinking in the exhilarating maleness of him. Only when she arched against him and felt the hard, throbbing centre of his masculinity did she draw back, opening her eyes with a shocked gasp.

Her green gaze met Gil's black one through a smoky screen of sensual longing, and her body trembled, as if it had found itself on the brink of a dangerous precipice and pulled back just in time.

'I...' she moaned softly, but Gil's fingers came up to still the sound, brushing against the swollen fullness of her lips and making them part again in helpless longing.

'Tell me. Are you involved with anyone?' he demanded mercilessly.

She couldn't lie. 'No,' she denied on a tremulous sob.

Then his mouth was on hers, infinitely persuasive, infinitely compelling, and soon, as the rhythm of his kiss consumed her once more, Olivia melted herself to him. On tiptoe she pressed against him, striving to ease her own urgent yearnings.

It took a few seconds for her to realise that Gil was easing her away from him. She shivered. She'd been consumed with heated passion and now she felt limp and drained... and fretfully unfulfilled. Her pale, delicate features were flushed and bright and her hair a tousled mass of curls around her head.

He lifted one lean finger to her lips, allowing it to stroke them briefly before sliding it down over the gentle tilt of her chin to the graceful arc of her throat and further to the exposed valley where the zip of her tracksuit-top stopped to reveal the gentle curves of her breasts.

Olivia felt the breath catch in her lungs and a gasp of pleasure murmured in her throat. A languid heat stole through her limbs and she stared at Gil in bemused anticipation. Please don't stop, she wanted to say. Her imploring gaze begged him to continue the journey, to somehow ease the tormented straining of her breasts against their lacy prison.

His head tipped back and he watched her through half-closed lids, saw desire cloud her eyes until their vivid green turned to opaque aqua.

'You have a very sexy body,' he murmured appreciatively, 'but I really don't think this is the time for lovemaking. You have work to go to and so do I.'

Lovemaking! How could any time be the right time for her and Gil to make love? And yet how could anything which felt so right be wrong?

He tilted her chin so she was forced to stare up at him. 'Though how the hell I'm going to sit at my desk and get any work done when I imagine all the things I'd rather be doing to you I don't know.'

Olivia's cheeks flooded with crimson. What things? She hardly dared think about them.

Gil gave a low, sexy laugh. 'Why the blush, Olivia? Or have you had very unimaginative lovers until now?'

The crimson turned scarlet and she couldn't manage a single word in reply.

Gil's fingers gripped her shoulders. 'This is only a postponement, though, Olivia. You know that, don't you?'

She nodded weakly, admitted at last the depth of her own need.

'Dinner...tonight?'

'Yes...please.' How could she deny what she wanted...needed so badly? She needed Gil. She'd needed him for the last five years but she hadn't been able to admit it until now. No other man affected her as he did. He seemed to know instinctively so many things about her. How... where to touch her. How to cause her senses to explode with pleasure, where her body's resistance was at its weakest. It made his power over her frightening.

And later, as she stepped into the shower, Olivia realised just how intense was the stabbing need which Gil had aroused in her. A need which she suspected only he could satisfy.

That evening, Olivia took almost as long choosing her dress as she had done on the morning of that outing in London five long years ago. If anything, this occasion seemed even more important.

Finally she selected a rose-pink evening dress; its modest style and discreet cut emphasised her femininity without flaunting it. She pulled her hair back into a chignon, leaving a few tendrils to curl loosely around her face to soften the effect. Pearl earrings matched the tear-drop pendant which nestled just above the valley of her breasts.

The appreciative look in Gil's eyes when he came to collect told her that the time and effort she had taken had been worthwhile.

'You look very beautiful,' he told her softly.

'Thank you,' she murmured, feeling her own stomach contract as she took in Gil's powerfully attractive presence. In a black evening suit, he looked bigger and taller than ever.

The restaurant Gil had selected was small and exclusive and definitely not the place to bring a casual friend. Small tables, lit by candles, were discreetly arranged, according privacy to the intimate glances and gestures which passed between many of their occupants.

Olivia wasn't quite sure what to make of Gil's choice. As a relative stranger to London, had he perhaps not realised that this was a restaurant whose main clientele were couples and would-be lovers?

'You don't approve?' Gil picked up on her mute observations.

Olivia shook her head. 'No, it's lovely. I just couldn't help noticing that all the other diners are...are couples,' she finished reluctantly, wishing belatedly that she hadn't commented on it at all.

Gil glanced round and then back at her, his expression faintly amused. 'And we aren't?'

Olivia felt herself blushing. 'Not...not in that sense.'

'What sense?'

Olivia knew she was getting herself into deeper and deeper water and wished now that she had never embarked on this conversation.

When she remained silent, Gil lifted one dark brow and regarded her quizzically. 'After this morning, can you still be in any doubt about our relationship?'

How could she help but feel bewildered by the abrupt change from antagonism to passion in their relationship?

Her own hostility had only been a protective device, a way of stopping him getting too close.

She had realised it as soon his kiss had swept that protection away.

But what of Gil's feelings for her? He wanted her. However sexually innocent she might be, she knew that much, but did that wanting extend to anything more than the urge to satisfy a physical appetite?

She made a small, inadequate gesture with her hands. 'This morning was so...so sudden.'

'It may have been sudden but it was hardly unexpected,' Gil said drily. 'What happened between us was inevitable. You know that, don't you?'

As he spoke, his fingers brushed against the length of her forearm as it rested on the table, seeming to draw all her nerve-endings to each spot where his skin touched hers.

As a demonstration of what he meant by 'it', his caress was more effective than any words. Was this what they called sexual chemistry? Olivia wondered dazedly. This dangerous excitement which was like a crackling fire burning ever more fiercely between them?

At last she nodded. 'Yes, I know,' she admitted softly.

Gil's eyes glittered in the candle-light and Olivia felt a tremor run like a feather down her spine.

Gil was a mystery to her in so many ways. There was so much about him she didn't know and couldn't yet ask. About Susannah Whitlow, for one. But that would come, she told herself. For the moment it was enough just to be with him and to know that he wanted to be with her.

The rest would surely follow if she could only be patient.

When the waiter arrived to take their order, Olivia barely skimmed through the menu. In truth, she hardly cared what she ate. Her insides seemed to be performing such strange contortions that she wondered if she'd be able to eat anything at all. In the end she chose light fish dishes which at least sounded easily digestible.

Over dinner it seemed as if Gil deliberately steered the conversation away from less personal topics, discussing their tastes in music and the theatre and comparing productions in New York and London.

At first Olivia found his change of mood disconcerting. It still felt strange and almost unreal to be sharing a meal with Gil at all, let alone swapping views on the arts, but gradually she found herself relaxing a little.

This was something of the man she remembered from five years ago and she was reminded of the qualities which had first attracted her to him—not just physically but mentally and emotionally. She responded to Gil on so many different levels. Was it any wonder that she still loved him?

The spontaneous thought came so swiftly and suddenly that Olivia felt the breath catch in her throat.

When she was eighteen, that love had been easy to admit to, but now, five years on, she was terrified to be even thinking it. It had made her vulnerable once and she dreaded being hurt by it a second time.

But even as Olivia tried desperately to erect the barriers which would give her some protection the powerful force of Gil's presence swept them all down again.

Here, with him sitting just across the table from her, it was impossible to deny the truth of her feelings for him. She loved him and no amount of reasoning could change that.

Olivia frowned as she realised that Gil was asking her a question. 'Sorry, what did you say?' She felt a million miles away.

'I asked if you'd seen the latest Lloyd Webber musical.'

She shook her head dazedly. She'd barely drunk any wine but she felt almost drunk on the intoxicating discovery she had just made. 'No—that is, I don't think so.'

Gil looked amused. 'Is it my imagination or are you having difficulty concentrating?'

Had her distraction been so obvious?

He leaned towards her until his warm breath fanned her cheek and her nostrils filled with the rich scent of his aftershave. 'Would it shock you to learn that I'm having great difficulty concentrating?'

His eyes skimmed over her, dwelling with a brief look of envy on the spot where the solitary pearl nestled.

Olivia felt her breasts swell and harden with desire. She stirred slightly, shifting towards him. Excitement uncoiled within her and her pulse quickened.

'Why don't you go through to the lounge? I'll order us some coffee,' Gil suggested softly.

Olivia nodded, deciding that she needed its sobering effect. Her response to Gil was so powerful that it seemed almost beyond her control. Moving away from the table, she turned and bumped into one of the diners just getting up from another table.

His fingers cupped her arm, steadying her. 'Hi there,' he smiled.

Her thoughts preoccupied, Olivia smiled back distractedly. 'Thank you,' she murmured briefly, moving on.

'Do you know him?' Gil asked, his fingers splaying lightly over her back as he guided her to the doorway.

His touch sent a melting sensation right down to her toes, so potent that Olivia could barely summon the energy to shake her head. When Gil went to order the coffee, she was grateful for the few minutes' opportunity to collect her spinning thoughts.

The lounge was as discreetly arranged as the dining area, with small sofas and easy chairs set at angles to ensure maximum privacy.

Olivia deliberately selected a single easy chair for herself. It was difficult enough not to yield entirely to the reckless desires sweeping through her as it was. With Gil immediately beside her on one of the two-seater sofas it would surely be impossible.

When a hand came down lightly on her shoulder, she swung round, expecting to find Gil. It came as something of a shock to find herself staring into the deep blue eyes of the man from the restaurant.

'Hi again. Olivia Beaufort, isn't it? Don't you remember me?'

Olivia frowned. 'Should I?'

The man laughed. 'Perhaps not but it would have been a lot better for my ego if you had. I'm David Castle. We met at Annabel Levington's party a few months ago.'

'The fancy-dress party?'

'The very same. I went disguised as a bottle of salad dressing, which could account for the fact that you didn't immediately recognise me.'

Olivia laughed too as she recalled that particular evening. 'You could be right. You did look a little different. I seem to remember that you had rather a well-known trade name emblazoned across here—' She reached up and lightly touched her forehead.

'And you said if I ever needed a good advertising agency to get in touch.'

'I did?'

'You certainly did. I've been out of the country for a little while or I'd have taken you up on the offer sooner. Am I too late?'

Olivia knew he was referring to her relationship with Gil and smiled gently. 'I'm afraid you are.'

David gave a good-humoured shrug. 'Just my luck!' He paused. 'But, since you are in the advertising business, perhaps you and I could get together to discuss a promotional package for computers which my company's planning? I could do with some professional advice.'

Olivia looked sceptical but David raised his hand and said solemnly, 'Scout's honour. I really am talking business here. No strings.'

He looked so funny that Olivia couldn't help laughing. 'Why don't you give me a ring at work some time and we'll discuss it?'

He laughed too. 'All right. What's your number?'

Olivia took out a pen and paper from her handbag and scribbled the number down on it.

David glanced at it. 'Thanks, I'll be in touch next week.'

Olivia watched him go, a smile still playing on her lips, and then turned to find Gil watching her from the other side of the room. Her smile disappeared as she registered his cold, angry look.

'Gil…what's the matter? Is something wrong?' she asked urgently as he came and stood beside her chair, seeming to tower above her.

'Get your coat. We're leaving,' he said curtly.

'Leaving?' Olivia stared up at him in shocked surprise, not understanding what had brought about this sudden change. Where was the attentive dinner partner of only a few minutes ago? 'But I thought you were ordering coffee.'

'I changed my mind.'

His icy tone made it sound as if he'd changed his mind about a lot more than just the coffee.

'But why?'

His eyes narrowed and his pupils seemed to burn right into her. 'I don't like being lied to, Olivia. You said you didn't know that man yet you obviously do. Who is he? An ex-lover?'

Olivia gave him a stunned look. Who on earth was Gil talking about? David? 'No!' she denied in hurt bewilderment. 'I met him at a party a few months ago. I didn't recognise him earlier, that's all.'

'How convenient,' Gil said with derisive scepticism. 'Perhaps he's a prospective lover, then. That was your phone number you were giving him, I presume.'

'My telephone number *at work*. To discuss business,' Olivia said furiously as anger bubbled up inside her, momentarily blocking out the hurt.

'Don't play me for a fool, Olivia. I saw the way he was looking at you. It was obvious he wanted to discuss a lot more than business with you,' Gil said curtly.

'I'd already made it clear that I wasn't interested in anything else.'

'I only have your word for that.'

Olivia stared at him, not trusting herself to speak. She wasn't sure if she was about to yell at Gil, hit him, or burst into tears. 'And obviously that's not good enough for you,' she said stiffly. 'I'm going to call a taxi.'

'Oh, no, you're not. I brought you here and I'm taking you home,' Gil announced with grim determination.

She had two choices: to refuse and face a furious row with Gil right here, where their raised voices were already attracting some speculative looks, or to comply and at least retain some semblance of dignity.

Olivia took a deep breath, trying desperately to stifle the bitter wave of pain which swept through her. 'All right, then,' she agreed, tilting her chin though her eyes threatened to brim over with tears.

The night was bright and clear. A million stars seemed to be twinkling above them but Olivia was immune to the sky's beauty. All she could feel was the tight band of angry hurt which seemed to have wrapped itself so tightly round her that she could hardly breathe.

Neither spoke during the journey and Olivia was briefly reminded of that other journey home she had made with Gil, five years ago. Just like then, he had jumped to all the wrong conclusions about her and misjudged her. Why was he always so ready to condemn her?

She didn't know the answer. All she did know was that there was no future in a relationship where there was so little trust. After all the evening's sweet promise, that realisation was like a knife-wound deep inside her.

The silence wasn't broken even when the car drew to a halt outside Olivia's apartment block. She got out quickly, slamming the door shut and willing herself not to look back until she reached the entrance.

Once there, she turned briefly, but Gil had already gone.

The next morning, Olivia took longer over her appearance than usual. Not surprisingly, she'd slept badly and needed a much more liberal application of make-up than usual to disguise the effects.

She had no idea what reaction to expect from Gil when she met him at the office but, whatever their personal feelings, somehow they had to work together, not just for today but for the next two years. Professional pride alone demanded that she should appear as poised as possible.

She got to work early, hoping to have some time to compose herself before Gil arrived. But that hope was dashed when she went in and glimpsed him already at his desk.

He looked striking in a dark pin-striped suit and crisp white shirt, and Olivia felt a stab of pain so sharp that she almost let out a cry. Somehow, though, she managed to get to her desk and sit down, pretending to examine the paperwork.

Seconds later, Gil entered her office. He didn't say a word, merely walked over to the door which connected her office with her secretary's and triggered the lock.

Olivia stared at him. 'What are you doing?' she demanded.

'I want to talk to you.'

'You can do that without locking the door. What on earth's Susan going to think when she arrives?' Olivia babbled furiously.

'I don't give a damn what Susan or anyone else thinks,' Gil growled tautly. 'I want to talk to you and I don't want to be interrupted.'

His face had such a grim, forbidding expression that the further protests on Olivia's lips died away and she looked at him in stunned silence.

'About last night...'

'There's nothing more to say about last night.'

'Well, I think there is.'

Olivia stood up, shoving her chair back roughly. 'I really don't want to talk about it,' she said tersely, moving fast towards the locked door.

'Oh, no, you don't.' Gil grabbed her forearm.

'Let go of me.'

'Not until you've heard what I've got to say,' he said curtly, refusing to release her despite her struggles. 'Last night...I over-reacted.'

All the previous night's hurt and anger bubbled to the surface and Olivia knew she couldn't remain silent on the subject. 'Damn right you did. You as good as called me a liar.'

Gil's brows drew together. 'When I saw you with that man, I thought——'

'I know what you thought and you were wrong. He's not my lover...he's not anything to me,' Olivia blazed at him.

Gil stared at her, his eyes seeming to burn right into her, as if trying to see inside her head. 'I know that now. You were telling me the truth and I wouldn't believe you.'

'But why not?' It was Gil's stark refusal to believe her that had hurt so badly.

He shrugged impatiently. 'I was angry and I wasn't in any mood to listen to reason.'

'That's no excuse,' she flung at him, struggling in his arms.

'Dammit! Will you keep still for a minute and listen?'

'No!'

'No?' His fingers came up to cup her chin, effectively holding her still, his mouth hovered above hers and his dark gaze swept over her flushed features. 'Marry me, Olivia.'

The order, for it didn't sound like a request, was so sudden and unexpected that Olivia could only gaze at him in stunned surprise. 'What . . . what did you say?' she stammered at last.

'I asked you to marry me.'

'But . . . but why?'

Gil stared down at her, his pupils like two deep black pools which she could so easily drown in.

'Does there have to be a reason?'

She shook her head dazedly, hardly able to believe that this was happening. It all felt somehow very distant and unreal. 'I don't know . . . I think so . . . There has to be some reason,' she murmured.

Gil ran his fingers through his hair in a gesture of impatience. 'Why does anyone marry? There has to be a hundred different reasons. I want you . . . and you want me. We work well together . . . the last few weeks have shown us that . . . we're a good team. We like the same things, share the same interests.'

There was one word missing from the list yet it was the one word Olivia longed to hear. What about love? Didn't that feature in Gil's scheme of things? All the others, yes, they were important, but wasn't it love which made a relationship special enough for marriage?

'Is . . . is that enough, do you think?'

Gil shrugged. 'It's as good a basis as most people have and better than many. I think we could make it work.'

In the same way that he had made a business work? By proper planning and organisation? That was what he made it sound like. But surely marriage couldn't be treated like a business? This was to do with people and feelings, not reports and accounts.

A marriage without love was like a plant without water. How could it survive and grow?

Their eyes locked for a few brief seconds and then Gil's hands dropped from her shoulders, leaving Olivia feeling achingly bereft. His expression shuttered.

'You don't have to give me an answer straight away. Think about it.'

His tone was carelessly dismissive, as if he had merely been negotiating yet another business deal.

A shadowy thought darkened Olivia's thoughts briefly but she swept it aside and her fingers clutched at Gil's sleeve as he turned away. 'No... no! I don't have to think about it.'

'Well?'

'Yes, I'll ... I'll marry you.'

Her voice sounded oddly distant, as if it were coming from someone else, not her. But then everything about Gil's proposal felt unreal. She could still hardly believe it was happening. She had to pinch herself to make sure she wasn't still in bed, dreaming.

But if she thought about it longer, considered it more deeply in the cold light of day, would her answer be any different? She knew it wouldn't. For wasn't any sort of marriage to Gil better than no marriage at all? She'd lost him once, five years ago, and she couldn't bear the thought of losing him again.

As for love, surely that would come in time? For the moment, she had more than enough to sustain them both.

Gil lifted a finger and traced the length of her throat. 'Good. You won't regret it. I promise.'

Olivia shivered at the silky promise and then leapt back from him in a startled reaction as the door-handle suddenly rattled.

'What's going on in there? Are you all right, Olivia?' Susan's muffled voice sounded through the door.

Olivia smoothed a hand jerkily over her hair and went to open it.

Susan's face appeared suspiciously in the doorway. 'What on earth were you——?' She stopped abruptly as she saw Gil standing on the other side of the room. Her gaze slid from one to the other and then back to Olivia, a wry smile playing on her lips. 'Sorry. Hope I didn't interrupt anything,' she said, not sounding in the least apologetic.

It was Gil who answered, saying smoothly, 'No, your timing was perfect. You can be the first to hear the news. Olivia has just agreed to become my wife.'

Susan's mouth dropped. 'Your... your wife?'

Gil nodded. 'That's right.'

A big smile appeared on Susan's face. 'You two are getting married?'

Olivia nodded and Susan rushed over to give her a hug.

'Congratulations! When?'

It was Gil who answered. 'Next week.'

Olivia frowned. 'Next week? We can't possibly be married so quickly.'

'Yes, we can, by special licence.'

'But I can't get everything arranged by then.'

'Of course *we* can,' he soothed her protests, reminding her that the responsibility was not hers alone.

'I must go and tell Vanessa,' Susan said excitedly, disappearing out of the door.

Gil came to stand beside her, curving his hand round her waist and leaning down to murmur huskily in her ear, 'Besides, I really don't think I can wait any longer than a week. Can you?'

Olivia had to admit the truth to herself. However much her reasons for agreeing to this marriage might differ from Gil's, he was right about one thing. She really couldn't wait, any more than he could.

They were married the following Friday in a functional register office ceremony. It was fortunate, Olivia thought wryly, that she had never cherished any fantasies of floating down the aisle in a white dress with a string of bridesmaids attending her and a packed congregation looking on, for her wedding day was certainly not the stuff such dreams were made of.

They had both agreed there was neither the time nor the need for such elaborate festivities and Olivia had settled for a smart silk dress in emerald-green as her wedding outfit.

Now, sipping a glass of chilled champagne, her gaze wandered round the groups of people dotted about the room. Most of them she knew but a few were strangers to her and she tried to match faces to the names which had appeared on Gil's list of wedding guests.

One she recognised as being Brad Langton, Gil's second-in-command at Rossaro Advertising. He had flown over especially for the wedding. Who was the striking brunette with him? she wondered.

'Everything all right?' Gil asked, coming to stand beside her.

'Yes, fine,' Olivia lied. She felt anything but fine. The strain of the last week had frayed her nerves to the point where she now felt that only sheer will-power was holding them together.

All the practical arrangements had gone according to plan, as Gil had said they would, but there had been no place in his strict schedule for the loving intimacies she had hoped would precede their wedding.

There had been few opportunities for talking, let alone reassurances, and now Olivia felt oddly tense and nervous, as if she were standing beside a stranger rather than the man who had just become her husband.

When she'd seen Gil at the register office, her heart had seemed to stop beating for a few moments. In a pale grey tailored suit, he had looked devastatingly attractive, and Olivia had felt her heart swell with love.

She had smiled tentatively but he had merely inclined his dark head briefly in greeting before ushering her through to the registrar.

'Have you looked at the wedding gifts?' he enquired now.

She nodded with a false brightness. 'Yes, there
are some lovely things, aren't there?'

Inside she felt like screaming. Why were they
talking like this—like two strangers, making
polite small talk? They were man and wife, for
God's sake.

'Those water-colours will look lovely in
your——' she hastily corrected herself '—our
apartment.' But Gil appeared not to notice her
mistake.

'I'm sure you're right,' he agreed coolly.

He sounded bored and distracted and Olivia's
heart sank. Was he already regretting a proposal
made in a moment of recklessness? she wondered. But if he hadn't wanted to marry her, why
had he let things go this far? Surely he would
have called the wedding off?

She thought of the whirlwind preparations that
had gone into the planning and organisation
during the past week: arranging the licence,
sending out invitations, booking this hotel, the
lavish party the agency's staff had organised on
their behalf. Had Gil too been so caught up in
the arrangements that he hadn't realised his
mistake until it was too late?

She pinned a smile on her face as she glimpsed
Brad Langton and his companion making their
way across the room towards them.

Brad was a plump, middle-aged man with a
wide, friendly smile. He pumped Olivia's hand
and beamed into her face. 'Congratulations, Mrs
Rossaro; Gil's a lucky man.'

Olivia's smile became a little more natural as she sensed his genuine warmth. 'Thank you,' she murmured. 'It was good of you to come at such short notice.'

Brad laughed. 'I wouldn't have missed Gil's wedding for the world. To be honest, I never thought I'd see the day. At Rossaro Advertising we all assumed he was a confirmed bachelor. But now I've met you I can understand why he changed his mind.'

His good-humoured courtesy was just what Olivia needed and she felt her spirits lift a little. She was letting her imagination run away with her, seeing slights and rebuffs where probably none was intended. This was her wedding day for goodness' sake. She should be enjoying it.

She turned to Gil, all the love she felt for him lighting up her face, and then hesitated as she realised that he hadn't even been listening to the exchange between her and Brad.

He was engrossed in conversation with Brad's companion. She was laughing at something he'd just said and her hand was resting lightly on his arm in a gesture of familiarity. It was very clear that they weren't strangers to each other.

Olivia felt a shiver run down her spine and for a moment she felt like an intruder, as if Gil and this woman were the wedding couple and she the guest.

Gil must have sensed her appraisal because he broke off what he was saying and turned towards her, saying lightly, 'Olivia, let me introduce Susannah Whitlow.'

Susannah Whitlow? Then Olivia remembered—this was the woman who had been Gil's personal assistant at Rossaro Advertising. The woman who she guessed had once been his lover. She struggled not to let her shock show.

Susannah was wearing an elegant designer outfit which was quite stunning on her tall, slender figure. She looked the way a PA should look: very smart, very efficient, and very capable; but although her mouth curved obligingly as Gil introduced them there was no warmth in the blue eyes which gazed into Olivia's.

The two men started to chat together and Olivia was forced to concentrate her attention on Susannah. She extended her hand politely. 'Hello,' she said, forcing her voice to sound neutral.

Susannah took it lightly, her touch icy. 'We spoke on the phone a couple of weeks ago,' she said unnecessarily.

Olivia didn't need reminding. 'Yes, I remember. You used to be Gil's PA at Rossaro Advertising.'

Susannah nodded. 'That's right. I suppose you could say you've taken my place. Only I didn't do quite as well out of it as you. I didn't marry the boss.'

Olivia could almost feel the hostile vibrations coming from the other woman. She was appalled by Susannah's rudeness but somehow managed to keep her temper and ignore that last remark. 'Who do you work for now?' she asked, attempting to change the subject.

'Brad, but it's not the same.'

'Why not?'

Susannah gave a brittle laugh. 'Need you ask?' she demanded as her eyes slid sideways to Brad's tubby frame, obviously comparing it unfavourably with Gil's leanly muscled physique.

'Brad seems a very nice man,' Olivia said loyally. He'd been kind to her when she needed it and she wouldn't forget that.

'Oh, he is. But niceness isn't everything, is it?'

'I think it counts for a lot, especially in an employer,' Olivia said coldly.

Susannah smiled, revealing gleaming white teeth which somehow managed to look more menacing than attractive. 'Do you think you'll find Gil equally *nice* now you're married to him? He is still your boss, isn't he? Won't it be strange working for someone who's also your husband?'

'I don't expect it to change anything.'

'Don't you?' Susannah's tone made it sound as if Olivia was being incredibly naïve. 'Let's hope you're not in for any unpleasant surprises, then.'

Olivia stared at her, disliking her intensely. But beneath the dislike and anger there was fear as well. Fear of what? she wondered bleakly. The fear that Susannah might be right?

'Speaking of surprises, we all got quite a surprise at Rossaro Advertising when we heard about the wedding, didn't we, Brad?' Susannah used the brief lull in the men's talk to bring them back into the conversation.

Brad smiled. 'I said that to Olivia earlier. A pleasant surprise, I hasten to add.'

Olivia noticed that Susannah didn't endorse that last addition. It was blatantly obvious that the news of Gil's marriage had come as anything but a pleasant surprise to her. Why was she so bitter about it? Because she'd hoped Gil would marry her?

'Where's the honeymoon? Or is the destination secret?' Susannah enquired with studied carelessness.

It was Gil who answered, saying coolly, 'We aren't taking a honeymoon. Beaufort's is handling several new client accounts at the moment and they can't be left to take care of themselves.'

It was what she and Gil had agreed, but still Olivia felt disappointed that they weren't going away on their own, even for a short time. Would it have been any different, she wondered, if he had loved her? Would he then have insisted on at least a few days' privacy just for the two of them?

Susannah was evidently pleased by the news. She fluttered her long black lashes at Gil, saying huskily, 'You mean you're actually putting work before play, Gil? As I remember you always managed to do both in equal measures... and both equally well.'

'I still do, I assure you,' Gil said smoothly.

'I believe you,' Susannah purred.

'I'm sure Gil and Olivia will manage to get away together later in the year,' Brad said stoutly, as if he sensed the veiled undercurrents running through Susannah's words.

Olivia certainly sensed them and she flashed Brad a grateful smile. But why hadn't it been Gil who'd made the response? Why hadn't Gil made it clear that the delayed honeymoon was a necessity, not a preference? Unless that *was* how he viewed it.

Suddenly Olivia didn't want to listen to any more of Susannah's barbs and sly innuendoes. She'd heard enough already. With a briefly murmured apology, she made her excuses and slipped out along the corridor to the ladies' cloakroom.

Once there she dampened a tissue under the tap and then held it to her eyes. She wasn't crying but she knew from the raw, burning sensation in her throat that tears weren't far away.

Whatever else, she mustn't cry. She wouldn't give Susannah Whitlow the satisfaction of seeing that she had reduced her to tears. Why had she let the woman get to her like this? Susannah Whitlow was obviously jealous and determined to do whatever she could to spoil her wedding day. She knew that, so why couldn't she just ignore what she'd said?

Olivia knew why. She was already too full of her own bleak misgivings to withstand Susannah's barbs as well.

'Ah! So this is where you've been hiding.'

Olivia hadn't heard the door open and she glanced round now to find Susannah standing in the doorway. The brunette's gaze went to the damp tissue in Olivia's hand but there was no sympathy in her expression, only a kind of smug satisfaction. 'Crying already? And you've only been married a couple of hours.'

Olivia felt like throwing the whole wad of wet tissues in her face. 'I'm just tired,' she murmured, wishing Susannah would go away.

But Susannah clearly had no intention of going away. She came into the cloakroom and shut the door behind her and then leaned back against it, as if to block anyone else's entrance.

'Was there something you wanted?' Olivia asked pointedly.

'Yes, I thought it would be a good idea if you and I had a little chat.'

Olivia disliked the sound of that intensely. 'We've already *chatted*,' she said coldly.

Susannah shrugged. 'A private chat, I mean. Just the two of us.'

Olivia didn't want to hear this. She knew instinctively that whatever Susannah had to say wasn't going to make pleasant hearing. 'Whatever you have to say, you can say in front of Gil. I don't have any secrets from my husband,' she said stiffly.

Susannah's laugh was as brittle as breaking glass. 'Maybe not, but he has a few he keeps from you.'

They stared at each other in silence. The cruel thrust was so sudden and unexpected that Olivia's hand clenched sharply on the damp tissue, causing droplets of water to trickle through her fingers. 'What do you mean?'

'Come on, surely you don't really believe this marriage is going to be the stuff of happy-ever-afters? He doesn't love you. You know that, don't you?'

Olivia blanched. Susannah's goad was too close to home. It echoed too many of her own misgivings of the last week. How could she know that Gil didn't love her unless . . . unless he'd told her so? No! Olivia shook herself. Gil wouldn't have done that.

'Of...of course Gil loves me.' She tried to give conviction to the lie.

'Has he told you that himself?'

Olivia longed to say yes, but it was like trying to paper over a wall with a huge crack in it and her numb silence was more eloquent than any words.

Susannah's look was gloating. 'So if you know he doesn't love you, you must have asked yourself why he married you.'

Of course Olivia had asked herself that question. Every night during the last week, she had gone over and over it in her mind but hadn't been able to come up with any more satisfactory answers than the ones Gil had given her himself. He desired her...wanted her...and thought they could make a life together. It was not the best basis for marriage, she knew that, but surely, she had reasoned, it was enough to build on.

Every instinct told Olivia to walk away from Susannah Whitlow right now, before she could drop any more poison in her ear. The woman was nasty and vindictive and obviously jealous. But some invisible force held her rooted to the spot. It was like self-inflicted torture but she had to hear what Susannah had to say. 'And why do you think Gil married me?' she asked at last.

'I *know* why he married you,' Susannah corrected her. 'You're part of a business deal, that's all.'

She eyed Olivia up and down as if she were a slab of meat on a butcher's block. 'You're a fairly attractive part of the package, I'll grant you that. I can see the appeal.'

Olivia didn't know whether to feel more stunned or insulted. Her brain didn't seem to be functioning properly. She felt as if she'd just received a crippling blow. 'Part of a business deal...what business deal?' she said dazedly.

Susannah smiled coldly. 'It's really very simple. Gil wants control of Beaufort's and what Gil wants, Gil gets. But he likes it to be sooner rather than later. Marrying you has speeded up the process considerably.'

'What are you talking about?' Olivia whispered.

Susannah took a lipstick out of her handbag and peered in the mirror. She wasn't going to rush. She was enjoying herself too much. 'Gil's been wanting to expand into the UK advertising market for some time and Beaufort's is an obvious choice. By marrying you, he's effectively got control of it. I'm sure he'll have no difficulty persuading you to use *your* shares to *his* advantage.'

Olivia felt the blood draining from her face. 'I don't believe you. Gil wouldn't marry someone just for the sake of an agency. No one would. It's ridiculous. Besides, if Gil wanted a UK agency, he could afford to buy one.'

'Yes, but Gil doesn't want just any UK agency. He wants Beaufort's. He always felt his step-father was badly treated by your grandfather, cut out of the will and all that. It's a family thing, you see, a question of pride. It has to be Beaufort's. No other will do.'

Desperation swept over Olivia. She searched for some other reason, any reason, to deny what Susannah was saying. 'But marrying me doesn't make any difference. I only stand to inherit thirty-five per cent of the agency's shares. He would need over fifty per cent to gain control.'

Susannah shook her head and tutted. 'You obviously don't know a great deal about your husband's business affairs. Gil already owns twenty per cent of the shares.'

Olivia's nails dug into the palms of her hands. She didn't believe this, did she? Her voice sounded unnaturally high-pitched and quavery. 'It...it's not true. You're lying. I would have known.'

One of Susannah's perfectly arched brows lifted. 'Would you? How? From the list of shareholders? They're listed under the name of a representative, of course, not his own name. Gil's good at keeping secrets. And not just about his business interests. Do you know what he was doing last night?'

Olivia went icy cold. 'He was at a meeting with Brad Langton.'

'Brad? Is that what he told you?'

Olivia felt a sick churning in the pit of her stomach.

'Gil dined with me,' Susannah said.

'You?'

Susannah's eyes turned glacial. 'Yes, me. It's not so surprising, is it? Not when you consider that I shared his office for five years and his bed for two. Your marriage isn't going to change anything, you know.'

She let that sink in, watching Olivia's horror with obvious pleasure, and then yawned conspicuously. 'The evening went on very late...very late indeed. If you were waiting for Gil to come to you last night, you must have had a very long wait. He didn't leave me until the early hours of the morning.' She opened her handbag and took out a small white card. 'Here's the hotel's telephone number. Call if you don't believe me.'

Olivia held out her hand for the proffered card in stunned silence. She gazed at it without managing to read a single word printed on it. She wanted to retch as that last knife-thrust found its target. Oh, God! How could he? How could Gil have slept with another woman the night before their wedding?

There was a sharp click as Susannah snapped her handbag shut, patently delighting in the pain she knew she had caused. 'I thought you should know the truth. Romantic dreams are all very well in glossy brochures but they don't transmit well to real life. Gil may be your husband but you'll never be the only woman in his life.'

'How...how do you know that I'm not going to go now and tell Gil all this?'

Susannah shrugged. 'I don't. But I'd make a shrewd bet that it's not likely. With that colour hair, you've got your fair share of pride and temper, I'd say. You won't like admitting you've been made a fool of.'

Moments later, Susannah Whitlow was gone and Olivia stumbled to one of the chairs and sat down. She felt ill. Her whole body was aching and sore.

She couldn't think straight. What should she do now? Go downstairs and carry out her threat, confront Gil with Susannah's vile accusations? That was what she wanted to do. She wanted to beg him to tell her it wasn't true, any of it—to tell her it was all a pack of lies.

But what good would a scene like that achieve? Even if he did deny it, how could she be sure that he was telling her the truth?

It suddenly dawned on Olivia how little she really knew about the man who had become her husband. She had thought that love and trust went hand in hand but now she felt as if she couldn't be sure of anything any more—least of all, Gil's motives in marrying her.

CHAPTER SIX

By THE time Olivia returned to the reception, Susannah had gone, apparently pleading a headache.

'It came on quickly. Jet lag, I expect,' Brad said lightly.

Jet lag? Or the effects of a sleepless night? The night she'd spent with Gil, Olivia thought, almost wincing as pain shot through her.

'She said to give you her best wishes.'

'Did she?' Olivia said coldly.

Brad gave her a quizzical look. 'Are you all right? You've gone a bit pale yourself. Would you like me to fetch Gil?' He glanced across the room to where Gil was standing with some guests from Beaufort's.

'No...no, don't bother him. It's nothing,' Olivia said hurriedly. The last thing she wanted was Gil rushing to her side, playing the part of a solicitous husband. Because that was all it would be—play-acting, she thought bitterly.

Somehow she managed to get through the rest of the reception, smiling woodenly and responding in dull monosyllables to everything that was said.

She couldn't look Gil in the eye, certain that he would be able to read the pain and distrust in her own. She hardly spoke to him either, knowing that once she started she wouldn't be able to prevent the torrent of Susannah's vile invectives and accusations spilling out.

Eventually, though, the final toasts were over and she and Gil were making their way out to his Jaguar in the car park. Hurriedly she slammed the door shut on the last goodwill messages as they rang mockingly in her ears.

As the car turned into the tree-lined road, Olivia rubbed her finger tips to a throbbing temple.

'Tired?' Gil asked. She nodded silently, steeling herself not to respond to his concern. 'Why don't you try and get some rest?' he suggested.

How could she rest when her mind was in such turmoil? Yet somehow it was easier to accede to Gil's suggestion than confront him with her fears. Thus she settled back in her seat and turned her face towards the window, away from him. Her mind veered wildly in all directions. She desperately wanted to believe that what Susannah Whitlow had told her wasn't true.

The woman was jealous that Gil had cast her aside for someone else, and was prepared to go to any lengths, sink to any depths, to spoil their wedding day. That was one possible explanation and Olivia tried to cling to the forlorn hope that it was the correct one.

Yet Susannah had spoken so convincingly, with such cool assurance, that surely there *had* to be some truth in what she had said.

It didn't take long to reach Gil's apartment block and Olivia found herself wishing the journey wasn't over. As the car glided silently down the ramp into the underground car park, she panicked.

What on earth was she going to say to Gil?

When she opened the passenger door, a few stray pieces of confetti fluttered out, the colourful strands turning wet and dull as soon as they came in contact with the ground. Olivia stared down at them, thinking how they seemed to symbolise the way the whole day had been ruined.

Neither spoke as they travelled up in the lift to Gil's penthouse apartment, but when his hand splayed lightly over her back to guide her down the corridor Olivia instinctively shrank from his touch, unable to bear even that slight contact.

She saw his gaze darken fractionally. 'Are you all right?' he asked quietly.

'Of course. Why shouldn't I be all right?' she snapped.

'You seem ... tense.'

'I'm tired, that's all.'

Gil's lips tightened but he bit back whatever reply he was about to make, merely opening the door to the apartment and then standing back to allow her to precede him in.

'Why don't you go and change?' he suggested, closing the door behind them.

'Slip into something more comfortable, you mean?'

Gil's eyes narrowed. 'Not in that sense, no. For God's sake, Olivia, what's the matter? You're like a cat on hot bricks.'

Olivia turned abruptly away from him and went through to the living area. 'I think I will get changed,' she said, glancing down at her outfit with distaste. She didn't think she would ever be able to wear the dress again. It felt tainted now, along with everything else that belonged to their wedding day.

Gil tilted his head back and watched her through lowered lids. His look was dark and speculative and Olivia wondered what thoughts were going through his head. Was he wondering if she suspected something?

She tensed, preparing herself, but when he spoke it was merely to say, 'All right. I'll fix us a drink. There's some wine in the fridge.'

Perhaps a drink would help. It might give her some Dutch courage at least. She nodded. 'Thank you.'

While Gil went through to the kitchen to get the drinks, she went to the master bedroom where her clothes were. She had brought all her personal belongings to the apartment during the previous week.

Then, unpacking her clothes, she had glanced at the huge king-size bed in Gil's bedroom and shivered slightly, excitedly anticipating the time when the two of them would share it. Now she looked at it and shuddered. He might not have slept there with Susannah but she couldn't get the image of the two of them together out of her mind. It made her feel sick just to think about it.

There were other bedrooms in the apartment. She would use one of those for the time being, until she decided what to do.

But first she had to tell Gil her intention. The breath caught in her throat as she imagined his reaction. He would be furious, she knew that.

With swift, vigorous movements, Olivia pulled out a pair of trousers and matching sweater from the wardrobe. They weren't what she had planned to wear this evening but the silky nightwear she had bought especially would be thrown away along with her dress. She never wanted to see any of them again.

Back in the living-room, she went to stand by the window, staring out into the inky blackness and watching the city traffic wind its way along the street far below. She didn't hear Gil come up behind her until his hand furrowed beneath her hair to caress the nape of her neck gently. She jumped as if she had been stung and his hands went to her upper arms, turning her round to face him.

'You've been as nervous as a kitten ever since we left the reception. What's the matter, Olivia?' he said quietly.

Now... now was the moment to tell him, to confront him with what Susannah had said, but somehow the words stuck in her throat. She simply couldn't bring herself to say them. 'Aren't all brides supposed to be a little nervous on their wedding night?' she said tersely.

'Some, maybe, but I would hardly have thought a display of virginal modestly was necessary in your case,' Gil replied drily. 'You don't have to pretend for my sake, Olivia.'

'Why are you so sure it is a pretence?' Olivia bit out sharply.

The angles of Gil's face tautened. 'Isn't it?'

But she couldn't tell him the truth about that either. Not now. 'Yes, it's a pretence,' she said flatly.

Gil's fingers moved upwards to knead her shoulders and she trembled convulsively. 'You are nervous, aren't you?' he said, sounding surprised. 'Don't be. We're going to be good together. I promise.'

The silky pledge was like a feather brushing against the full length of Olivia's spine and she knew she couldn't bear Gil to be in such close proximity. His nearness affected her senses, scrambling them into frantic disarray until she couldn't think straight.

'I'm hungry,' she said, ducking beneath his arms and moving away from him. 'Do you think we could eat?'

'All right, if that's what you want.'

'It is,' Olivia said quickly.

Suddenly Gil gripped her forearm and pulled her back to stand in front of him. 'What's making you so jumpy? Are you frightened I'm going to rush you? You needn't be, you know.'

Olivia felt herself blushing and closed her eyes against Gil's scrutiny. No need to ask what he was talking about. 'No... No, I'm not frightened,' she denied, unable to hold his gaze.

She hadn't realised before what a good actor he was. He looked as if he genuinely cared but in truth he didn't care at all. How could he lie so blatantly? How could he profess concern when all the time he'd only married her for her shares? She was a commodity to him, that was all.

Gil let his hand drop. 'I'll sort out the food.'

But Olivia shook her head. 'Why don't you go and take a shower? I'll start on the food.'

She knew Gil thought she was acting strangely but she didn't care. Before she confronted him with what Susannah had said, she needed to make a telephone call, and for that she needed to be alone.

A few minutes later, Olivia took out the card which Susannah had given her and dialled the number of the London hotel. She asked the receptionist to confirm that a Mr Brad Langton and a Miss Susannah Whitlow were booked in. They were. And whether Miss Whitlow had dined there with Mr Gil Rossaro the night before. Her face blanched as she heard the affirmation.

'Didn't Mr Langton join them?' she asked with a hint of desperation.

There was a moment's pause as the receptionist checked, then, 'No, they dined alone.'

Olivia's fingers trembled so much that she could barely replace the receiver in its cradle.

So Susannah had been telling the truth. Olivia's heart felt like a dead weight in her chest and she realised how much she had been hoping and praying that the woman had been lying.

Suddenly she recalled the vague fear which had swept over her when Gil proposed, how she'd likened it to negotiating a business deal.

What a fool she'd been! That was all it ever had been to him—a commercial transaction. No wonder he hadn't mentioned love. Love had never even come into it.

Somehow she forced herself to go through to the kitchen and start on the food preparation. Earlier today, she had been looking forward to this moment; she had imagined her and Gil laughing and talking as they made the meal together, then sharing it over a candle-lit table. And after? She shuddered and deliberately blocked that image from her mind.

She had to think. Think hard and quickly. What should she do now? She could always leave and go back to her own apartment. She wasn't a prisoner here. Gil couldn't hold her against her will.

But neither could she imagine him just letting her walk out. Gil never gave up what he wanted without a fight. Somehow she had to find a way of playing him at his own game.

When he emerged from the bedroom some half an hour later, he had changed into thigh-hugging denims and a midnight-blue sweatshirt. Droplets of water glinted on his hair and Olivia winced at the sudden pang his appearance provoked. Would nothing kill the attraction he had for her? Was she destined to love a man who was prepared to use her so cruelly, for the rest of her life?

They talked desultorily over the meal but the tension was obvious. It was like a taut wire being stretched tighter and tighter between them, and Olivia felt that any minute she was going to snap.

Susannah had been right about everything—even her, she acknowledged bitterly. Somehow the woman had known that Olivia's pride wouldn't allow her to confront Gil with the truth, and she'd been right.

Olivia knew she couldn't bear to lose the little dignity she had left. All right, so Gil had only married her to get what he wanted out of this marriage. Well, somehow she was going to convince him that she had done the same.

'I thought you said you were hungry,' Gil said at last, setting down his own cutlery and watching Olivia rearrange her food yet again.

'I...I thought I was.'

'But you're not.'

'No.'

'What's the matter, Olivia? Why don't you try and tell me what's upsetting you?'

Olivia shut off her ears to his pretence of concern. It was a sham, that was all. A mockery. Just as their whole marriage was a mockery. She felt like screaming at him but somehow she managed to keep her voice low.

'I think I'll go to bed.'

Gil reached across the table and lifted her wrist, turning it over to rub it sensuously with his thumb.

'All right. You go and get ready. I'll join you soon.'

'No!' Olivia snatched her hand away.

The shrill denial seemed to hang in the air between them for several seconds before Gil said quietly, 'OK, Olivia, let's quit playing games. What's wrong?'

'Nothing...nothing's wrong. I intend to go to bed alone, that's all.'

Gil's eyes narrowed. '*That's all*? It's our wedding night and you want to sleep alone yet you say nothing's wrong?'

Abruptly he stood up and came round to Olivia's side of the table, pulling her upright to stand in front of him. Her breathing quickened as her pulse went crazy and the blood pounded through her head.

'You're tense. It's been a long, hard week.'

His fingers massaged the knotted muscles in her shoulders and it took all Olivia's resistance not to curve against him. It wasn't fair of him to do this, to sound as if he genuinely cared, when in truth it was all an act. He didn't care at all.

She struggled in his arms. 'That's got nothing to do with it. I'm not going to sleep with you, Gil.'

His hands dropped abruptly from her shoulders and he slid them into his pockets. 'Why?'

This was the moment that was going to require all her acting skills, if she was going to convince him that she was telling him the truth. He had only married her to suit his own purposes. Well, let him think she had done the same. 'I...I never intended this to be anything more than a marriage in name only. Eventually I'll seek an annulment.'

'An annulment?'

'That's right. I have no intention of consummating our marriage.'

'What?' The single word had a cold, metallic sound.

Somehow she carried on. 'I only married you because I needed you—not you personally, that is, but your shares. Your shares in Beaufort's.'

She paused, wondering if Gil would deny it, hoping even now that Susannah had lied and that he didn't possess the twenty per cent holding she had claimed.

But Gil's next words destroyed that hope forever.

'How the hell did you find out about them?' he demanded.

Olivia gripped the edge of the table for support. It was true, then. Gil did own the shares.

Pain swept over her and it took all her self-control just to remain upright. Tears burned the back of her lids but she wouldn't cry. She wouldn't let him see her misery.

Somehow she forced herself to say coldly, 'I made it my business to find out about them.'

'You had me investigated?' He said it deliberately, as if he couldn't really believe it. He sounded furious and disgusted, as if she'd done something abhorrent.

Olivia felt his violent reaction as forcefully as if he'd just hit her. She felt numb. No sounds would come from her throat.

'Did you?' Gil demanded again.

'I . . . I made certain enquiries.'

Somehow Olivia struggled to get the words out. 'Because . . . because I wanted to know if it was worth my while marrying you.'

The silence which followed was more menacing than any outburst might have been and Olivia's breath caught in her lungs as she waited to see what Gil was going to say or do. His dark eyes glittered savagely.

'Worth your while? What the hell are you talking about?'

Olivia knew she was trembling. 'In two years' time we'll own over fifty per cent of the shares between us. I . . . I'm sure we can use that to both our advantages.'

Olivia had never seen Gil so angry before; not even on that morning at her apartment had he looked quite as dangerous as this. The black expression which descended on his features terrified her.

But what right did he have to look so enraged? How dared he act like the injured party? His pride was dented, that was all. He'd only married her to get her shares yet he wasn't prepared to accept that her reasons for marrying him could be equally self-motivated.

'You're telling me that you went through a marriage ceremony just to give you a bit more muscle on the board? I don't believe it. What devious little game are you playing, Olivia?'

He didn't believe her. But then he wouldn't, would he? He wouldn't want to believe that she could have played as cruel a trick on him as he had played on her. It would hurt his pride too much.

Somehow she stood her ground. 'But it's not just a bit more muscle, is it? Our combined shareholding will be fifty-five per cent. It will be the majority holding.'

Gil took a step towards her. 'My God! I never realised you were such a scheming little bitch,' he said icily. 'Or let's just say I thought you'd changed. But I was obviously wrong. You haven't changed from that sly eighteen-year-old who went behind her grandmother's back to score cheap tricks at parties, have you?'

Olivia felt as if he had just slapped her. Her face burned scarlet. 'I hate you,' she spat at him and the next moment her arms were flailing against his chest.

Gil caught her wrists in a vice-like grip and shook her. She stared at him, her chest heaving as the air was dragged in great, savage gasps from her lungs.

'You don't hate this, though, do you?' he said as his mouth hovered above hers.

Olivia gasped as his tongue slid along her lips, moistening them. Almost unconsciously she opened her mouth, half in protest, half in shock at the curious sensation his touch aroused.

But Gil didn't wait to let her savour the moment. His mouth possessed hers, with a rough, aggressive passion which allowed no resistance or hesitation. It wasn't a seduction, it was an overwhelming assault on her senses. Almost unconsciously, in a response which had nothing to do with willingness, Olivia felt her mouth opening beneath his, felt herself inviting the invasion of his tongue, felt a dangerous, seductive heat seep through her body.

CHAPTER SEVEN

MOMENTS later, Gil swung her up in his arms and carried her through to the bedroom, setting her down on the bed.

'No...Gil...we can't,' Olivia protested dazedly, suddenly realising his intention.

'Why not?' he demanded roughly. 'You are my wife and this is our wedding night.'

She lay there for a moment on the bed, staring up at him, her breath coming in short, strangled gasps, and then watched with reluctant fascination as he slowly and deliberately removed his sweatshirt.

He came and sat down on the bed, one side dipping slightly beneath his weight. His fingers burrowed beneath her hair and curved round the nape of her neck, drawing her to him.

When her mouth was only inches away from his, he paused.

Olivia knew this was the moment to say no. If she said it now, Gil would leave her. He wouldn't force her against her will.

But somehow the time for that denial had passed. It had no place among the urgent desires which filled her. Her mouth lifted in silent invitation and when Gil's lips covered hers Olivia was filled with a curious sense of the inevitability of what was about to happen; Gil was going to make love to her. Now...here...tonight.

She loved him and that was all that mattered. Beaufort's ... shares ... Susannah Whitlow slid mercifully to some distant corner of her mind and her whole being was filled with the steady rhythm of his mouth as it moved over hers and the clever arousal of the hands which made her tremble convulsively.

Olivia felt herself slipping deeper and deeper into a labyrinth of sensual need, a labyrinth where only Gil knew the way through the tangled maze of passages. Hungrily she followed his lead, her instincts governed by the primitive desires which were sweeping through her. Her own touch grew bold. Her hands explored the lean body which stretched out alongside her, marvelling in the sculpted muscles which rippled beneath her fingers, hearing with delight Gil's breathing thicken as her fingers sought the smooth, hard planes of his stomach.

His hands went to her outer clothes and then to the silky underwear beneath, drawing away each item in turn until her body lay pale and gleaming before him. Gil gave a deep murmur of satisfaction as his eyes roamed freely over her nakedness, their black depths glittering sensuously.

Then he was stripping away the last of his own clothing, his body golden and magnificent as he lowered himself to her.

His hands moved to the cauldron of heat which was her belly, spreading that fire to her hips, her thighs until Olivia felt she was about to be consumed by its conflagration. She pressed against him. 'Gil ... please ... I need you ... now.'

Her thighs parted willingly as she felt Gil's body smooth against her own, seeking...wanting to feel him inside her. Yet despite that fierce wanting his first thrust made her tense in sudden pain.

Her eyes opened wide and she saw Gil's staring down into her own, a shocked dawning in their dark depths.

But by then it was too late. Olivia's need was too fierce for retreat now and she began to move against him as her body responded blindly to its own instincts.

This time, Olivia was barely aware of her infinitesimal withdrawal as Gil slid deep inside her, her own need making her arch against him in the quest for she hardly knew what. He was leading her up a mountain and with every step which brought her nearer to the peak Olivia's wonder grew. Then suddenly she was at its summit and a crescendo of exhilaration spilled through her, making her cry out with shuddering pleasure.

It was then that Gil's own control shattered and he joined her on the black, swirling mountain-top they had reached together.

Slowly, drowsily, Olivia floated back down to earth. Instinctively, in the lazy aftermath of love-making, her body sought to burrow into Gil's strength and warmth.

The sudden chill as he sat upright and shifted away from her caused a small moan of protest to escape from her lips. She opened her eyes to find him staring down at her, the cold, accusing expression on his face a shocking contrast to the heated intimacy they had just shared.

'I understand now why you wanted an annulment. After this, I guess you'll just have to settle for a divorce,' he said icily.

'A divorce?' She struggled to sit upright as reality flooded back with painful intensity.

'You were counting on your virginity to secure you an annulment, I presume?'

Olivia shook her head disbelievingly. How could Gil talk to her like this? Did what they'd shared not mean anything to him? Didn't it change anything?

'Please, Gil——'

But he bit off her plea with cold indifference. 'Don't worry. I'm sure you can come up with some suitably convincing lie. After all, lying's something you're very good at, isn't it?' With those bitter words, he stood upright, gathered up his scattered clothes and walked out of the room.

Left alone in the huge bed, Olivia felt too numb and horrified even to cry. She lay like a statue, unable to believe what had happened.

Had any bride ever felt worse on her wedding night? she wondered, as pain and humiliation clawed at her stomach.

Their lovemaking had meant nothing to Gil. But why should it? He neither loved nor respected her. There was no doubt about that now.

When Olivia woke the next morning, she lay motionless for several minutes. She felt sick and nauseous and a buzz-saw was squealing mercilessly inside her head.

She'd hardly slept; all night long, she'd been tormented by the memory of Gil's cruel words before he left her. Yes, she had lied to him, but only to protect herself. She hadn't deliberately set out to deceive him as he had done her.

She had some aspirin in her handbag but that was in the kitchen where she'd left it last night. Her ears pricked, trying to discern any sounds of movement in the apartment. Nothing. Gil must still be asleep.

She swung her legs noiselessly over the side of the bed and reached for her dressing-gown, pulling it tightly round her before opening the door and peeping out.

The other bedroom doors, further along the corridor, were wide open, but there didn't seem to be any sounds coming from the rooms. Olivia hesitated and then tiptoed cautiously along the passage.

She had to pass the other bedrooms to get to the kitchen and peered round each door cautiously, but every room was empty and so were the beds. After a few minutes searching, she realised that the whole apartment was empty. She was the only one here. Where on earth was Gil?

Suddenly a horrible thought occurred to her. Perhaps he'd left her. Just gone without a word. She sat down on a sofa in stunned silence, her body turning icy cold. Somehow she hadn't expected this. She hadn't expected Gil to give up without . . . without a fight. For her shares if not for her.

Where could he have gone? Not to Susannah. She and Brad had been catching a late flight the night before. Where, then? To a friend?

She jumped up and went over to the large desk in a corner of the room. There must be a diary, an address book, something that would give her a clue to his whereabouts.

She was just flicking through the contents of one of the drawers when she heard the front door open and then slam shut. Seconds later, Gil appeared in the open doorway and she almost jumped out of her skin. 'You nearly frightened me to death!' she exclaimed.

Gil's eyes flicked from her to the open drawer. 'I bet I did,' he said coldly. 'What's the matter? Haven't you had time to search under the floorboards yet?'

Olivia frowned. 'What——?'

'What the hell were you expecting to find? Something lurid and unpleasant? You're wasting your time, I assure you.'

Olivia coloured as she suddenly realised what he was talking about. He thought she'd been prying! In fact she could see now that he'd been jogging. 'I...I wondered where you were, that was all. I thought you'd gone. I was just trying to find a...a telephone number...or something...' Her voice trailed off as Gil lifted one disbelieving eyebrow.

'Forgive me if I find this description of wifely concern a little difficult to swallow.'

'It's true!'

Gil's laugh was black and humourless. 'You admitted last night that your wedding vows were a pack of lies. After that, do you really expect me to believe anything you say?'

No more than his had been! Olivia thought furiously, hating the way he kept trying to make out that the deceit was all on her side.

'I haven't lied about everything,' she retorted.

'No? There was certainly one crucial piece of information you omitted to mention—the fact that you were a virgin. Or was it all part of your devious plans? To keep it secret until you wanted an annulment and then *produce* it, like a hidden weapon?'

He made her lack of sexual experience sound like something cheap and nasty and Olivia hated the way he made her feel so humiliated. 'Don't be ridiculous.'

'Well, if you did it's too late now,' he said drily. 'I don't think even your carefully laid plans took into account what happened last night.'

Nothing in her life so far had prepared her for what had happened then. In all her wildest dreams, she had never imagined that making love to Gil could be so wonderful. But neither had she ever imagined the pain and despondency which would follow in its wake.

Her angry look was only a cover for the pain she felt inside. 'Last night doesn't change anything.'

'No, it doesn't,' Gil agreed sardonically but as he spoke his eyes slid downwards.

Olivia suddenly shivered and wanted to clasp her arms round herself. But not for warmth, for protection. 'I...I'm going to go and get dressed,' she said abruptly.

Gil angled one hip against the door-frame. 'I'm not stopping you,' he drawled.

Not physically, no. But to get out of the room she was going to have to go right by him and he obviously had no intention of moving aside to let her pass. Self-consciously, Olivia moved towards him. When she reached him, she paused. 'Can't you move?' she demanded breathlessly.

'Why? Isn't the ice maiden quite as sure of herself any more?' Gil's insolent tone made it clear that he had no intention of moving out of her way.

It was impossible to get past without touching him and Olivia felt her body grow hot as it came up against Gil's. Her face flushed crimson as memories of the previous night's lovemaking flooded back into her mind.

She half expected him to bar her exit and draw her to him. Half expected it and, for a few mad seconds, half wanted it too. But he made no effort to restrain her and as she slipped down the corridor towards her bedroom Olivia cursed the disappointment which swept through her.

Olivia stared at the hands on her watch. It couldn't be nearly two o'clock in the afternoon, could it?

It must be. When she'd got back to her room, she had lain down on the bed for a while, trying to work out what she should do. Through sheer exhaustion, she must have fallen asleep.

Her mouth felt dry and despite the aspirin her headache felt no better. She wondered if she could be coming down with something...if flu wouldn't be preferable to the knowledge that it was Gil who was making her feel so ill.

She couldn't live like this; she realised that now. She couldn't live a lie. Pride had made her lie to Gil last night about her reasons for marrying him but she'd been a fool to think she could keep up that kind of pretence.

For her their lovemaking had been wonderful. She'd even been foolish enough to think it could change things between them, but she'd been wrong. Gil's cold manner afterwards had told her that. If he'd cared for her at all, he couldn't have just got up and walked away from her. But he had.

Despite everything, she still loved him, but she had to face the fact that he didn't love her and never would. Living with him would be like self-inflicted torture. She couldn't bear it.

The decision made, Olivia decided to see Gil straight away and tell him she was returning to her own apartment. She dressed hurriedly and found him at his desk, a heap of papers spread out in front of him.

'You're ... you're working,' she said unnecessarily.

'Yes.' He looked as if he might have been in his office at Beaufort's, dealing with important business and irritated by the interruption. 'Do you want something?'

Olivia swallowed. 'Yes...I've decided this isn't going to work ... us living together, I mean ... I've decided to return to my own apartment ... tonight.'

The words came out in a rush. There'd been no time to prepare some kind of well-presented speech.

Gil sat back in his chair, watching her. 'Are you suggesting that we separate?'

Separate? It seemed such a ridiculous term to use when they'd spent so little time together. Did one night and a day count? 'Yes...separate,' she agreed dully.

Gil didn't seem shocked by the suggestion, only mildly surprised. 'Why the change of mind? You seemed certain enough yesterday of what you wanted from this marriage.'

'I...I thought I was.'

'But now you're not.'

'No...yes.' Olivia shook her head. She couldn't think straight any more. 'I don't want anything from it.'

'Not even an increased shareholding?' It was a sceptical taunt.

Olivia felt like screaming. She thought she could bear anything but this kind of cruel sarcasm. 'No, not even that,' she said tightly. 'I don't care about the shares any more. I just don't want to have to live with you any longer.'

'Then it's a pity you didn't think about that before you married me,' Gil said coldly.

'What do you mean?'

'Have you any idea how Beaufort's will be affected if you and I separate now?' Gil demanded.

Olivia shrugged. 'It won't be good for the agency, I know that, but——'

'It will be disastrous,' Gil interrupted her tersely. 'It would jeopardise all the new accounts and lose us God knows how many existing ones. Who the hell is going to have any faith in an agency where the managing director and the

major shareholder separate within days of
marrying? Beaufort's would be a laughing-stock
in the City.'

Olivia blanched at Gil's stark description. Was
it really as bad as that? 'But I don't want us to
stay married,' she said desperately.

Gil gave a sardonic laugh. 'And you think I
do? Do you think I want to remain married to a
woman who openly admits that she only married
me to enhance her shareholding? I've already
considered the options and separation is not one
of them. Not unless you want to be left with a
majority shareholding in a bankrupt business.'

So Gil had already considered separation?
Irrationally the knowledge hurt. 'Perhaps I'm
prepared to take that chance,' she said with a
touch of defiance.

Gil gave a cool nod. 'Perhaps you are. Perhaps
the future of Beaufort's doesn't matter quite as
much to you as I thought it did. But there is
another consideration... a more personal one.'

Olivia had no idea what he was talking about.
'What's that?'

'After last night, you could be pregnant.'

The suggestion was so unexpected that Olivia
felt her knees grow suddenly weak. 'Pregnant?'
She repeated the word as if she'd never heard it
before.

Gil's eyes narrowed. 'I know you were a virgin
but you must be aware of the connection between the sexual act and pregnancy. The latter
is often a consequence of the former,' he
added drily.

'I don't need a biology lesson,' Olivia said
tautly, still shocked by the possibility of what Gil
was suggesting. 'It isn't likely, surely?' she murmured, half to herself.

'I didn't say it was likely, merely that it was a
possibility. Given that consideration, perhaps you
should wait a while before making any hasty
decisions.'

He said it so clinically, as if they were at a
board meeting, not talking about something as
personal as a baby... their baby.

Despite everything, Olivia experienced a
sudden flare of wonder that perhaps, even now,
a new life could be growing inside her. Unconsciously her features softened and when she
looked at Gil again she found him watching her
with a strange expression on his face.

She smiled tentatively, she couldn't help it, but
if she'd hoped for some response from him she
was disappointed. If anything the gesture seemed
to make him more distant than ever. Within
seconds, his face was a cool, expressionless mask.

He sat forward in his chair, glancing down at
the papers on his desk, as if to indicate that her
allotted time was almost up. 'I suggest that for
the moment we maintain the appearance of
having a normal marriage. It would certainly be
in the company's best interests. As for the possibility of your being pregnant, we will have to wait
and see. Are you in agreement?'

What choice did she have? After everything
Gil had said, it seemed the only option. She
nodded, wishing it didn't seem like such an impossible task.

*   *   *

Olivia got her first taste of just how difficult it was going to be very quickly. As soon as they walked into work on Monday morning, Susan and Vanessa greeted them with beaming smiles. They obviously thought it very romantic to have a newly married couple working together and sharing adjoining offices.

'Did you have a good weekend?' Olivia enquired politely of Susan as soon as she had settled down at her desk.

'Not half as good as yours, I'll bet,' Susan said laughingly.

Olivia tried to smile in return but the facial movement involved felt stiff and unnatural. 'Did you get those letters typed?' she asked quickly.

Susan nodded. 'They're ready for your signature. I'll go and get them.'

Just as she returned, Gil appeared in the adjoining doorway. 'Are you free for lunch?' he asked.

It was on the tip of Olivia's tongue to say no, she wasn't, when she remembered Susan's presence. 'Of course,' she said with forced lightness.

His next words made it clear that he wasn't proposing a romantic tryst. 'I'd already arranged to lunch with Jack Beesham today but he heard about our getting married and he's just been on the phone to invite you along too.'

'How lovely,' Olivia lied.

'One o'clock, then. We'll go together,' Gil said briefly before returning to his office.

'What a pity,' Susan whispered. 'I bet you'd much rather have lunched with Gil alone rather than having to sit through a stuffy business lunch.'

If only Susan knew the truth, Olivia thought despondently. She hated having to deceive her like this. They'd worked together for a long time and this sham felt like a betrayal of their friendship. In all honesty, the last thing she wanted was to be alone with Gil. 'I really don't mind Jack Beesham coming along,' she said truthfully.

'You're very understanding,' Susan said sympathetically. 'But I suppose you and Gil have got to put the agency's interests before your own wishes.'

It was almost too close to home for comfort. What would Susan say, Olivia wondered, if she knew that she and Gil were *only* staying together for the sake of Beaufort's? And maybe for the child they had conceived? Olivia hastily pushed that possibility aside. It was still too new and too fraught with problems for the future which she had no idea how to deal with.

At one o'clock precisely, Gil came into her office.

'Are you ready?'

She nodded, feeling her stomach contract with tension as soon as he spoke to her. Would she be able to eat any lunch? she wondered in sudden panic.

'I've ordered a taxi. It'll give me a chance to brief you on Jack Beesham during the journey.'

Olivia frowned. 'I'm sure I've heard the name before.'

'You should have. He owns one of America's biggest fast-food outlets. He's dealt with Rossaro

Advertising in New York for several years and now the company are expanding into the UK market he's considering appointing Beaufort's for the publicity launch.'

Olivia sensed that this was a vital contract for Beaufort's to secure—not only lucrative but prestigious as well. But why had he particularly wanted to meet her? Was it simply down to good manners that he had invited her to lunch or was there some other reason?

'Jack Beesham's a highly respected businessman,' Gil explained briefly once they were seated in the taxi. 'But he's also a committed family man. He's well-known in the States for his stance on moral issues affecting marriage and children.'

'Meaning?'

'Meaning that he's expecting to meet a pair of adoring newly-weds,' Gil said drily.

'Surely you're not suggesting that our relationship has anything to do with whether or not he appoints Beaufort's for the campaign?' Olivia asked sharply.

Gil shrugged. 'On pure package presentation, no. Of course Jack will go for the best deal. But if it comes to a toss-up between us and another agency our "happily married status" might just help us clinch the deal.' He spoke with heavy sarcasm, making it clear what a sham that term was when applied to them.

Olivia bunched even further into a corner of the seat. 'I hate this deceit,' she said tensely.

'Do you?' Gil slid her a sceptical look. 'I'd have thought you'd be used to it by now. You seem to practise plenty of it.'

Olivia clamped her mouth shut on the retort which leapt to her lips and stared fixedly out of the window. She refused to be drawn into yet another slanging match with Gil. His determination to make her out to be the guilty party in this whole mess, and refusal to acknowledge his own blame, infuriated her. But hurling insults at each other wouldn't alter anything.

The taxi stopped outside a small Italian restaurant and they got out. While Gil paid the driver, Olivia walked through the door and into the reception area. She glanced round, taking in the tasteful décor, and then almost jumped out of her skin as she felt Gil's fingers curve on her waist.

'Relax, darling. It's me, your husband, remember,' he said lightly. Olivia glared at him. 'Don't grimace, sweetheart; it doesn't suit you.'

His hand still resting easily on her waist, he guided her into the restaurant's interior, where a tall, distinguished-looking man was already rising to greet them.

'Jack, let me introduce my wife, Olivia. Olivia, Jack Beesham.'

'Delighted to meet you.' The man shook her hand warmly.

Olivia smiled politely. 'Thank you.' She forced herself to concentrate on Jack Beesham rather than on Gil's fingers, which seemed to be lingering on her waist far longer than was necessary.

She felt enormously relieved when they sat down and the heated band across her skin where he'd touched her grew cool again.

'I understand congratulations are in order.'

Olivia swallowed. 'Yes, that's right.'

'Only married a few days? You and Gil should be off on honeymoon somewhere, not talking business.'

'We'll take one later, when the agency's a little less busy,' Gil said easily.

'Be sure you do,' Jack instructed, laughing. 'In fact, if you take my advice, you'll take one every year. Dorothy and I have managed to notch up twenty-seven years together so it must be a good recommendation.'

Twenty-seven years! What would he say if he knew that she and Gil hadn't even managed to make their marriage work for twenty-seven hours? Olivia wondered unhappily.

Somehow she managed to get through the meal, contributing to the business details where appropriate and trying to respond to Gil with suitable wifely affection. But every minute which passed was an ordeal and Olivia longed for it to be over so that she could wipe the falsely bright smile from her face.

Jack Beesham was a nice man...a sincere man, and she hated deceiving him like this. Was it really worth it? Even for Beaufort's? At one time she would have considered almost any sacrifice worth paying for the agency, but now she wondered if the price wasn't just too high.

CHAPTER EIGHT

THE next couple of weeks were the worst Olivia had ever known. Previously, even when her personal life had been unsettled, she had always been able to rely on work to boost her spirits.

But now even that escape route had been closed to her. Work provided no more refuge than home did. Home? That was a joke. How could the apartment she shared with Gil possibly be called a home? A home was somewhere you felt relaxed and comfortable, but Olivia never felt anything but tense and uneasy while she was there.

Her aversion to being there meant she spent more time than ever at work, but since she must, even at Beaufort's, work alongside Gil there was no respite.

None of the staff knew the truth about their marriage and Olivia was finding it increasingly difficult to play the part of new bride with any conviction.

She tackled every task that Gil set her with dogged efficiency but took little pleasure in any of it. She found herself scrutinising all faxes and letters which passed between Beaufort's and Rossaro Advertising with suspicion, searching for evidence of communications between Gil and Susannah Whitlow.

Susannah Whitlow! The name sent a cold, angry shiver down her spine every time she thought about it. Did she and Gil correspond? she wondered with an icy hatred. Did they exchange whispered conversations on the telephone? Her imagination ran riot as she conjured Susannah's husky laugh rippling down the line, telling Gil exactly what they would get up to when they did get the chance to meet.

It had been a hard day at work and Olivia just wanted to get back to the apartment and have a long, hot soak in the bath. What made such a prospect particularly appealing was the knowledge that Gil wouldn't be there. He had flown over to Paris for a meeting and wasn't due back until after midnight.

Susan and Vanessa, Gil's secretary, had already left and Olivia was just packing up to go when he walked through the door of her office. She stared at him in shocked surprise. 'I thought you were in Paris.' It was more of an accusation than a greeting.

'Missed me, darling?' he mocked, eyes gleaming.

She gave him a mutinous look. He seemed very pleased with himself. Why?

'You're not leaving, are you?' he demanded, shrugging off his jacket and setting his briefcase down on the desk.

'It is after six o'clock,' she pointed out.

'Good. That gives us about six hours.'

Olivia frowned. What was he talking about? 'Six hours to do what?'

'Put together a presentation for Légère Foods, the French dairy product manufacturers. They're planning to introduce a new yoghurt to Britain but they haven't appointed an agency yet. If we can get something to them by tomorrow morning, we're in with a chance.'

'Tomorrow morning?' Olivia stared at him. 'We can't possibly put something together by then.'

But Gil was already taking papers out of his briefcase and spreading them out on his desk. 'Not a full presentation, no, but we can put together a credentials presentation. It will give them some information about Beaufort's and our existing work. If they like the look of us, they might just invite us to submit a formal pitch for the account.'

'What do you want me to do?'

It had taken only seconds for Olivia to realise that Gil was absolutely serious. This wasn't her husband speaking, this was her boss, and professional loyalty demanded that she support him every step of the way. If he was prepared to spend the evening working on such a long shot, then so was she.

'Here's some information about the product.' Gil slid some leaflets across the desk towards her. 'Have a look through them and see what work we've done before which might tie in with it.'

Quickly Olivia set to work, sifting through files to find the sort of data Gil wanted. It was a time-consuming task and a couple of hours had gone by before she even realised it.

The building grew quiet as the various departments shut down for the night. Outside the city traffic hooted and roared but it seemed a million miles away, as if she and Gil were cocooned in their own small world.

'Is this the sort of thing you're looking for?' she asked at last, taking the accumulated folders over to his desk.

They went through them together as Gil's quick, incisive mind approved some for inclusion and dismissed others.

'Why not that one?' Olivia demurred as Gil rejected a series of magazine shots. They were for a dairy product too and Olivia thought the soft, pastoral scenes they re-created were appealingly romantic.

'Uh-uh.' Gil shook his head. 'That's not the sort of image this company is aiming at. They're targeting this product at the young, keep-fit career woman, who wants a snack that's both healthy and fashionable. This sort of presentation isn't hard-hitting enough for them.'

'OK, I understand,' Olivia nodded. 'What about this?' she suggested, picking up on his line of thinking.

Gil nodded. 'Perfect. That's exactly the sort of thing we're looking for. Good girl. See what else you can find that's similar.'

By ten-thirty, Olivia was exhausted, but she refused to let Gil see how tired she was. He had not let up, not for one minute, and she knew he'd been on the go far longer than she had. A car had arrived to pick him up and take him to the airport at six o'clock that morning. She knew because she'd lain awake in bed and listened to him go.

'Why don't I go and get us some coffee and sandwiches from the delicatessen on the corner?' she suggested.

Gil nodded, then sat back in his chair and raked his fingers through his hair in a weary gesture. 'That's a good idea. But get one of the porters to go with you. I don't like the idea of your being out on the streets alone at this hour.'

A sudden warm rush of pleasure swept over her and she wondered fleetingly what it would be like to be cherished and protected by Gil's strength and concern all the time.

Just as quickly she thrust the treacherous thought aside. Gil would have said as much to any of the female employees. There was nothing special about his making the remark to her.

Half an hour later they had demolished the coffee and sandwiches and Olivia wondered when any meal had ever tasted as good as that snack. They'd talked about the presentation while they ate and for the first time since their marriage there seemed to be no barriers between them. They weren't two adversaries but two people with a common bond and goal, and for that short time it changed everything between them.

It made Olivia realise how things could have been if... She sighed. 'If wishes were horses, beggars would ride'. What was the point of wishing things were different? They weren't and that was that. No amount of wishing was going to change anything.

An hour on and Gil finally pronounced the presentation complete. 'Or at least as complete as it can be given the limited time we've had to work on it,' he modified. 'Thanks, Olivia; I couldn't have done it without you.'

Flustered by the compliment, she made a big pretence of sorting out the chaos on her desk, letting her dishevelled curls fall across her face to hide the blush which scalded her cheeks. 'That's all right,' she murmured. 'I'm only doing my job, after all.'

She didn't hear Gil moving across the room to stand beside her. Not until his lean, muscled frame was so close to hers that she was forced to look at him. He was watching her oddly and she wished she knew what he was thinking. She wished...she wished so many things. All of them impossible.

'No, that's not all you're doing. You work damned hard and you don't just work in a job, you work *at* it. There's a difference. I like that degree of commitment. I respect it.'

Olivia's blush deepened. She had no idea how to deal with Gil when he was being nice to her. It seemed to throw her more than any threats or arguments. In her confusion, she turned quickly and stumbled against a filing cabinet. She might have fallen altogether if Gil's hands hadn't shot out to catch and steady her.

'Are you all right?' he demanded.

She probably would have been if he would have just let go of her. As it was, she didn't know if it was slipping, or his touch, which was making her tremble so violently. 'I...I think so,' she nodded.

'You're shaking...and you've gone very pale. Are you sure you're all right?'

'I'm just tired.'

His eyes narrowed on her face. 'You're sure that's all it is?'

Olivia frowned. 'What do you mean?'

'Do you know yet whether you're pregnant?'

The question made Olivia tremble even more violently. She couldn't seem to stop. 'I . . . I don't know yet. I don't think so,' she murmured. She'd pushed the possibility to the back of her mind during the last couple of weeks, hardly daring to think what the consequences would be if she was.

They stared at each other for a moment and then Gil pulled her into his arms. His hand went to her head, cradling it on his shoulder and his fingers stroked her hair. 'Sssh...it's all right. Stop shaking.'

For a moment she resisted but his warmth and strength seemed to envelop her and she found herself curving against him, feeling herself grow still beneath his soothing touch.

Afterwards she wasn't quite sure when the tempo changed. But suddenly she knew that Gil's stroking caress had ceased to be comforting and was awakening a quite different sensation inside her. The candle-flame had been transformed into a fiercely burning fire which sparked responses throughout her body.

Warm breath fanned her cheek as she dragged her eyes up to his face and from a long way off she watched as his mouth moved closer and closer to hers. Seconds stretched into aeons as she awaited his kiss, then sought the hard possession of his mouth, and finally submitted utterly to its compelling pressure.

His hot tongue licked the inside of her mouth, probing its sweetness, and promising more until soon a dangerous excitement was licking along her veins, blocking out the timid rationality of thought and sweeping away all reason. Her hands eased their way up to his neck, combing possessively into the thick crispness of his hair and unashamedly drawing him closer until her cheeks, her nostrils and her mouth were saturated by the feel, breath, and touch of him.

One of Gil's hands shifted from her hip to the back of her dress, unpeeling the zip so that cool air inched its way the full length of her spine. But not for long. Gil's fingers sought the opening he had created and began to move over her skin with warm, sensuous caresses. She arched against him, trying to evade the hot, sweet havoc his touch was creating.

The delightful ravishment of her mouth deepened and the hand which hollowed her back moved downwards over the soft roundness of her buttocks, drawing her to him and arousing her even more with the evidence of his own arousal.

Slowly her dress slipped from her shoulders but Olivia no longer cared. She was past caring, past thinking. Her whole body was shaking, gripped by the need which only Gil could arouse in her. He arched her backwards and his mouth sought the warm, creamy swell of her breasts, nuzzling each swollen curve in turn until Olivia thought she was going to faint with pleasure.

'Olivia, come home with me now,' Gil muttered roughly against her skin.

Olivia didn't give herself time to think, time to ponder the consequences, time to change her mind. She did exactly what she wanted to do. She nodded, meeting his kiss eagerly. 'Yes, oh, yes, Gil. Let's go home.'

Home! She'd never called his apartment that before. Never felt as if it was her home. But now, tonight, would change that.

Their departure from the office was not a break in their lovemaking but rather both a prelude and a sequel. While Gil pulled her dress back up over her shoulders, his mouth dropped tiny, devouring kisses on her face. His caresses wooed her, making her tremble and yearn for the moment when he would take her in his arms with no barriers between them.

They were almost at the door when the telephone rang, its shrill noise intrusive and unwelcome in the midst of their honeyed whispers.

Leave it, Olivia wanted to urge, but she knew that Gil could not ignore it. It might be something relating to the presentation they had been working on. Thus she made no protest when he withdrew the arm which had encircled her shoulder and moved away.

She leaned back against the door-frame, smiling as she watched his tall, lean body walk across the room, and thought how much she wanted him, how much she loved him.

'Susannah?'

That single word and the odd look which Gil cast backwards over his shoulder in her direction were sufficient to break the spell.

Olivia stared at him, a look of horror dawning on her face. Susannah Whitlow! Was this the time they had agreed for their secret telephone trysts? A time when no one else was normally around? Gil often worked till midnight at the office. She knew why now. No wonder she hadn't found any evidence of their communicating; they only carried out their business during the hours of darkness.

She felt sick, sick to her very core. She couldn't hear the muttered words that Gil was saying and she didn't want to. All she wanted was to get away from him...from them, because it felt as if Susannah Whitlow had just become a physical presence in the office between them.

Somehow Olivia managed to get out of the office and into the corridor without Gil hearing her. She was at the lift when she heard him calling her name. But he was too late. She had no intention of waiting to hear what he had to say, of listening to his lies.

She slumped into the lift and pressed the button for the ground floor. It seemed to take ages but she knew that it was much faster than taking the stairs. Even if Gil had bothered to do that he couldn't catch her now.

At the bottom she paused briefly at the night porters' office.

'Do you want me to call you a taxi?' one of the men offered, seeing she was alone.

Olivia shook her head. 'No...no. It's all right. I'd rather walk.'

Outside the cool night air hit her like a weapon. She felt as if she'd been blind drunk, and going outside had instantly sobered her. She had been drunk, she thought bleakly, drunk on sex and lust. Because that was all there was between her and Gil: sexual chemistry. It didn't matter that she loved him; it was just a one-way feeling. It wasn't reciprocated.

Her legs felt weak and spongy but somehow she made them move, one in front of the other. She didn't care where she was going, as long as she got as far away from Gil as possible. She didn't feel any fear about being on the city streets so late at night. She felt too horrified by what had nearly happened to be afraid.

She had no idea how long she'd been walking when a car drew up alongside her. At first she was too lost in her own thoughts to even be aware of it but then she sensed it slowing down and stopping. For the first time a *frisson* of fear made her shiver. Where was she? She didn't even know which direction she'd been walking in. Deliberately she kept her eyes firmly ahead of her, only walking faster when she heard footsteps behind her on the pavement. She was being followed!

Then a hand fell on her shoulder and she was swung round. Horrified, she stared up into the face of her assailant. She was about to scream when his face moved out of the shadows and into the moonlight. Gil!

Her heart felt like a wild bird beating in her ribcage. 'You nearly scared me to death,' she yelled at him.

'Good! You're bloody lucky to have got away with a scare,' he snarled at her. 'What the hell did you think you were doing running out on to the streets like that?'

His face looked very black and threatening in the darkness and Olivia's throat contracted in fear. He grabbed both her shoulders and shook her. 'Answer me, damn you. I've been cruising the streets looking for you. I think I deserve some sort of explanation.'

So, he thought he *deserved* an explanation, did he? What about Susannah Whitlow? Was he going to *explain* about her? She was so angry that her voice came out shrill and tight. 'I didn't ask you to follow me.'

Gil's grip on her forearms tightened and his voice was dangerously cold. 'Don't be so bloody childish. What the hell did you expect me to do? Leave you to roam the streets all night?'

Olivia felt as if she was about to explode. Her fury was like a tight band around her chest. 'Why should you care?' she demanded angrily.

'Don't let's play games, Olivia.' Gil's mouth twisted. 'We both know what we started back there and we both know that we wanted it to end up in bed. Don't try to deny it. What I want to know is what changed *your* mind. When I answered that phone, you bolted out of the door as if the devil himself were after you. Why?'

As if he needed to ask. What had he expected her to do? Politely wait until he'd finished his conversation with his mistress and then fall meekly into his arms? God, he was arrogant! 'What was Susannah Whitlow doing, phoning you up at that time of night anyway?' she demanded.

'What the hell has that got to do with——?' Gil broke off suddenly and his eyes narrowed. 'You can't be jealous of Susannah.' He sounded as if he were half talking to himself.

'Of course I'm not jealous of Susannah.' The denial came out a little too quickly and a little too vehemently.

Gil stared at her. 'You are, aren't you?'

Olivia wondered if she dared bite his fingers to release herself and decided she dared not. 'No, I bloody well am not,' she snapped.

Suddenly Gil's expression changed. He looked vaguely amused, as if he had accidentally stumbled on something unexpected but very useful. '"The lady doth protest too much, methinks."'

'Why should I be jealous of her?' Olivia babbled wildly.

'Don't ask me to explain the mysteries of a woman's mind. Men put two and two together and get four; women invariably arrive at five,' he said grimly.

'And they're often right,' Olivia said tersely, resenting the way Gil was making it sound as if she were the one jumping to all the wrong conclusions. She'd reached the right ones. He just didn't like it. 'What did she want anyway?' she bit out.

'It was a business call.'

'At this time?' It was a sceptical taunt.

'It was only early evening in New York,' Gil pointed out.

'But midnight here.'

'Susannah used to be my PA. She knows I often work late.'

'That's not all she used to be, is it?' Olivia said bitterly, the words bursting out before she could stop them.

They stared at each other in silence then Gil frowned. 'If I told you that Susannah and I had an affair but that——'

'I don't want to hear this.' Olivia struggled violently in his arms. She didn't want to hear the details of Gil's relationship with that woman. Not now. Not ever.

Gil shook her. 'Why not? Why don't you want to listen to the truth?' He pushed her back against the wall. 'I'm going to tell you this and you're going to listen whether you like it or not. Of course I've had previous relationships, other lovers. I'm thirty-three years old, dammit! But it was over between Susannah and me before I came to England. It's in the past. It's got nothing to do with you and me.'

Olivia had to fight the desperate yearning to believe him. Oh, God! How she wished it were true. If only they were talking about a relationship which was over and done with. But they weren't. Gil's relationship with Susannah wasn't over. He'd slept with her the night before their wedding.

Maybe she could have forgiven him the rest, but not that. Never that. Her stomach felt as if it was full of knives, every one of them tearing her to pieces. Her eyes were bright with unshed tears as she stared up into Gil's face.

'So you didn't see her the night before our wedding?'

One word, that was all she wanted to hear, but she knew it was the one he could not give.

The silence hung between them for several seconds and then suddenly she thrust against him with her fists, taking Gil by surprise. She wrenched herself away from him, ran to the road and flagged down a passing taxi. She half expected him to come after her but he didn't. He let her go.

And somehow that thought was the one which hurt the most. He had let her go. The tears which had been brimming fell in hot, wet streaks down her cheeks and she balled up in a crumpled heap in the back of the taxi, hugging her pain and misery to her like a vice.

'Don't take on so, love,' the driver muttered sympathetically. 'He's not worth it.'

Olivia knew he wasn't worth it, but she loved him, and because she loved him it hurt. It hurt like hell.

Olivia had no idea where Gil spent the night and she didn't care—at least that was what she told herself. She knew he hadn't come back to the apartment; she knew because she had lain awake throughout the long hours of darkness, unable to sleep for the tormented thoughts going through her head.

This state of affairs couldn't continue between them; she realised that now. She should have confronted Gil on their wedding day and told him what she knew, told him then that she couldn't live with him after finding out the truth. It would have been painful but less so than the prolonged agony of the last few weeks.

She couldn't go on any longer. They would get a divorce, anything he wanted, just so long as they didn't have to continue with this living hell.

When she arrived at the office the next morning, she was taken unawares at finding Gil already there. His dark suit was freshly pressed and his white shirt crisp and clean. Wherever he had spent the night had evidently catered for his laundry requirements too. Was it a hotel, she wondered edgily, or did he have a British mistress tucked away in a discreet corner of London, as well as one in New York?

Gil looked up when she entered, his eyes raking over her with cold, deliberate insolence. 'I presume you got home safely?' he said curtly, making it sound as if the enquiry stemmed from a sense of duty rather than any real concern.

His hostility made Olivia crumple inside. She couldn't bear this steely anger. But what else had she expected? In truth she hadn't expected to see him here at all. If she had, she would have prepared her armour, the rigid defences she needed to face him. Without it, she felt exposed and vulnerable. She nodded wordlessly.

'Good! That means the apartment is empty. I'm going back there now to pack a bag.'

Olivia stared at him. 'Pack?' Was he leaving her?

Gil gave a harsh laugh. 'Only one bag, Olivia. Why the stricken look? Did you think I intended to move out? Isn't that what you want?' Then, as Olivia remained silent, 'Isn't it?'

Olivia didn't know how to deal with this brutal interrogation. Say yes, her brain told her, but somehow her mouth wouldn't obey the instruction. 'I...I don't know,' she faltered. 'Where...where are you going?'

'Does that matter?'

Was he going to Susannah? Was that what he was planning?

Gil's eyes narrowed, as if he could read her thoughts. 'And you can get rid of those ugly suspicions right now,' he said coldly. 'This has nothing to do with another woman, however much you may try and convince yourself that it does.'

Olivia didn't know why but she believed him. Wherever Gil was going, it wasn't to Susannah. 'Where, then?' she repeated. 'I...I need to know...I may need to contact you about agency business.'

'Vanessa has my number if that should be necessary.'

Olivia didn't relish the idea of having to ask Gil's secretary for the details of his whereabouts.

'But...but I'm——'

'My wife?' Gil supplied with cruel mockery, his black brows winging upwards. 'I want a flesh-and-blood woman to share my life, Olivia, not a scheming, jealous shrew. Since you have decided that your role carries no...duties...other than those of my personal assistant, then I think I am entitled to decide that it should carry no privileges either, other than those enjoyed by the rest of the workforce. If you want to know where to find me, you'll have to ask Vanessa—just as any other member of staff would.'

'You bastard,' she gasped, desperately hurt by his cutting description of her and by the humiliation he was proposing to impose on her. He knew how embarrassing it would be to have to ask Vanessa for that information.

Gil's eyes glittered. 'What did you expect, Olivia? That I would meekly allow this state of affairs to continue? That I would be content with a wife who blows hot one minute and cold the next? A wife who only married me to ensure her hold on the family business?'

Olivia gazed at him. How could he stand there and coolly accuse her of what he had done? Did he feel no guilt himself?

'But you——' She bit back on the terse admission and then wondered why she was hesitating. Why didn't she just tell Gil what she knew? Why didn't she confront him with the truth? All of it? It was what she had decided to do.

She ran her tongue over dry lips, as if to try to lubricate them and make them mobile. 'You——' she began, but Gil interrupted her with callous indifference.

'I have a plane to catch,' he said coldly, 'and my car is already at the entrance. Whatever you want to say will have to wait my convenience, not yours.'

Olivia recoiled as if he'd slapped her in the face. Gil couldn't have made it plainer how low she ranked in his order of priorities.

'Don't let me delay you, then,' she said, pride demanding that she match his glacial tone with one of her own.

'I don't intend to.'

Moments later the office door clicked shut with a dull, metallic sound, leaving Olivia feeling numb and frozen, as if some final barrier had just clicked into place between her and Gil too.

She could barely move, barely think; both actions were too painful. Somehow she managed to get to her chair and slump down in it. When the office staff arrived nearly half an hour later, she was still hunched in the same posture.

In a roundabout way, and without revealing the depth of her own ignorance on the matter, she managed to find out that Gil was flying to Paris to deliver the presentation they had prepared the night before, and then on to Japan, and wasn't due back until the following week.

She tried to be glad about his absence, telling herself that it would give her time to consider her options and make plans for the future. Plans which didn't include Gil. But reason was no match for the aching feeling of loss which overwhelmed her. She had never known it possible to feel such misery.

'Are you feeling all right?' Susan asked when she came in and found Olivia staring forlornly out of the window for the third time that morning.

Olivia shook her head. It was pointless trying to pretend that she felt fine. Her lethargy might not have a physical cause but she didn't know when she'd ever felt worse.

'You're not pregnant, are you?' Susan enquired gently.

Olivia felt herself burning bright red. 'No! Of course I'm not. Don't be ridiculous,' she denied.

Her secretary looked amused. 'All right, there's no need to be so touchy. It's a perfectly normal condition for a newly married lady. I was just wondering whether congratulations were in order, that's all.'

'Well, they're not,' Olivia muttered ungraciously, and felt immediately contrite. Susan was only being kind.

'I...I think I may be coming down with a cold or something,' she murmured, a little less harshly.

'Or something,' Susan agreed, with a wry glance in the direction of Olivia's abdomen, evidently not wholly convinced by her boss's assertion that pregnancy was not even a possibility.

'I told you——'

'I know...I know.' Susan held up her hands in mock defeat. 'Time will tell, as they say. In the meantime, why don't you take a couple of days off work? You look as if you could do with a break.'

Olivia shook her head. 'I can't. Not with Gil away as well. One of us should be here.'

'Vanessa and I can hold the fort for a few days.'

'Thanks for the offer, Susan, but I don't think so.'

'Well, let me know if you change your mind.'

'I will.'

In fact, later that day, Olivia's period came and she knew for certain that she wasn't pregnant with Gil's baby.

It should have been a relief. After all, she hadn't wanted to bear a child conceived without love or respect, had she? A child conceived in anger and suspicion?

Yet despite all her arguments she did feel a profound sense of loss. Perhaps she had hoped that a baby would bring her and Gil together... give them some hope of a future together. But now that hope had gone and Olivia knew that their marriage couldn't survive without it.

She and Gil had nothing to bind them together any more, except Beaufort's, and now she no longer cared what happened to the agency. Gil could have her shares, every one of them, and she would resign. Their last link would be severed.

She recalled Susan's suggestion that she should go away for a few days, and on the spur of the moment decided to do just that.

On Friday afternoon, she caught the plane up to Scotland. She desperately wanted to get away from London and anything that might remind her of Gil. She'd been planning to go up and check on the house anyway, and now seemed as good a time as any.

CHAPTER NINE

THE large grey stone building was just as she remembered it, stark and a little intimidating yet somehow well suited to its rugged surroundings. She hadn't been here for almost a year and yet nothing seemed to have changed. That had always been part of the attraction of the place; it was a timeless certainty in a constantly changing world. Perhaps it was because her own life was so deeply disturbed at the moment that she had felt the house's lure so strongly.

The grounds were a little overgrown, that was all, and Olivia made a mental note to ask Mr McDonald if he needed any extra help with the heavy work. Mr and Mrs McDonald lived in the lodge and had looked after the house and grounds since before Olivia was born. They were part of the house; she couldn't imagine a time when they wouldn't be here either.

Inside, most of the rooms were closed up, with dust sheets spread over the furniture. Olivia didn't bother to disturb them. The large kitchen was quite big enough for her needs during the short visit—that and her old bedroom. Going upstairs, she found that the bed had been made up and the room aired; the window was open and familiar blue curtains wafted gently in the breeze.

She had just finished her tour of the house when there was a light tap on the front door and

Mrs McDonald bustled in. She was a comfortably plump woman, in her late fifties now, and Olivia always associated her with the delightful aroma of newly baked bread and fresh apple pies.

They hugged warmly then Mrs McDonald held Olivia off to look at her. 'My wee lassie a married woman... I can hardly believe it. Is Mr Rossaro with you?' she enquired in her broad Scottish accent.

Olivia shook her head.

'Och, that's a pity. We were looking forward to meeting him. But never mind. Next time, maybe?'

Olivia nodded, trying to swallow the lump in her throat. Gil wouldn't be visiting the house— ever—but she couldn't tell Mrs McDonald that. The McDonalds were one of the happiest couples she knew; they would never comprehend the complex web of deceit and misery that she and Gil had managed to weave into their lives.

'I can't tell you how pleased Mr McDonald and I were when we got your letter telling us about the wedding. "You'll see", I said to Robert. "We'll have some wee bairns running about the place before very long. It'll be lovely to have some little ones around again".'

Olivia hoped that Mrs McDonald's fading eyesight wouldn't notice her eyes brimming with tears. First Susan and now Mrs McDonald! She supposed it was only a natural assumption on their part, but the mention of children was like a knife in her heart.

'You're not going to be here all on your own?' Olivia nodded and Mrs McDonald tutted. 'Will you not be lonely? Would you like me to come and sleep in a for a couple of days?'

'No, I'll be perfectly all right, honestly,' Olivia assured her.

'The telephone's not connected, you ken.'

'I know.' Olivia laughed. 'I'll just have to shout very loudly if I run into any trouble.'

'Well, if you're sure you'll be all right, I'll leave you to settle in. Anything you need, you just let us know. I've got some shopping in and there's a wee bit of supper on the stove. I'll pop back up in the morning and do a few chores.'

Olivia smiled affectionately as she watched Mrs McDonald set off back down the drive. She approved of the older woman's simple, uncomplicated view of life. Why on earth did her own have to be such a mess?

She sighed, closed the door and went down the corridor to the kitchen where Mrs McDonald had left an enormous stew simmering. Olivia supposed that was her 'bit of supper'. Good grief! There was enough to feed an army.

Mrs McDonald had obviously counted on Gil coming too. It was that thought which killed her laughter dead. She wondered what he was doing now and abruptly pushed the painful thought aside. He hadn't contacted her since he left. It had been Vanessa who'd informed her that he'd arrived safely in Paris and then in Tokyo.

There'd been no messages for her and she deliberately hadn't asked for any to be passed to him. Their separation already seemed a reality.

*   *   *

Quite unexpectedly, Olivia slept well and awoke the following morning feeling ready to face the day. From the moment she got up, she never stopped.

In the morning, she went round the house and grounds with Mr McDonald, checking on structural repairs that were needed and then contacting local tradespeople to authorise them. And in the afternoon she went for a long walk on the moors, revelling in the wind in her hair and the sun on her face. The heather was sprouting and the moors were turned into a sea of pure purple. It was so beautiful and so peaceful that she walked and walked until she felt as if she could drop.

It was how she wanted to feel. She hoped that if she drove her body to sheer physical exhaustion it would block out all other feelings.

That evening when she got back to the house she felt calmer than she had done in days. Her body glowed with the day's exertions and a healthy tiredness crept through her bones. All she wanted was a bath, then supper, then bed. She felt as if she could sleep for a week. She wished she could stay for a week but she had to get the plane back to London the following evening.

After towelling herself dry, she slipped on a long silk nightie and matching robe. There seemed little point in getting dressed again since she was alone in the house and had no plans to go out.

She'd just finished her supper when the knocker sounded at the front door. Olivia started and then checked herself. It would be one of the

McDonalds come to make sure she had everything she needed for the night. It was typical of their thoughtfulness.

She almost fainted when she opened the door and found Gil standing on the doorstep. 'What . . . what on earth are you doing here?' she stammered. 'You're supposed to be in Japan.'

'Well, as you can see, I'm not,' Gil said grimly, pushing the door open and stepping inside.

'You can't come in,' she told him, feebly trying to push against the solid muscle of his chest and failing to budge him one inch.

'I already am,' Gil said curtly and slammed the door shut behind him.

They glared at each other for several minutes. Olivia was so shocked by his sudden appearance that she scarcely knew what to think, let alone say. His business suit was rumpled, she noted. He looked as if he'd just spent a long time travelling.

'What are you doing here?' she demanded.

'I could ask you the same question,' Gil said roughly. 'Do you know how bloody difficult it's been to find you? No one knew where you were.'

Why had he gone to so much trouble to find her? Olivia wondered fleetingly. 'Susan had the address,' she told him.

'I found that out eventually. You still haven't told me what you're doing here.'

'I came to check on the house.'

'That's all?'

Olivia felt tired of fighting. She just wanted to get this over and done with. 'I wanted to get away from London . . . and from you. I'm leaving you, Gil,' she said dully.

Gil's expression was grim. 'Oh, no, you're not!' he said. 'Not without some kind of explanation.'

He didn't really want an explanation. All he really wanted was the shares. Well, he could have them, all of them. 'It's all right. You can have my shares, every one of them. I don't want them,' she told him.

'Neither do I.'

The retort was so quick that Olivia glanced at him in surprise. Why was he still playing games, pretending that wasn't why he'd married her? 'Yes, you do,' she said stiffly. 'You've wanted them all along. They're the reason you married me. You don't have to pretend any more.'

'What the hell are you talking about?' he demanded.

'Susannah told me everything, Gil. Please don't pretend you don't know what I'm talking about.'

There was a brief silence, then Gil frowned. 'Susannah? When did she talk to you? At the wedding?'

Olivia nodded.

A dull anger darkened his gaze. 'What exactly did she tell you?'

Why was he making her go through this? Was he deliberately trying to make it more painful? 'She told me about your shares in Beaufort's and how you needed mine to give you a control-ling influence.'

'You said that you already knew about those shares before we married.'

Olivia shook her head. She might as well tell Gil the whole truth. There was no point in lying now. 'I had no idea about your shares until Susannah told me about them at the reception. When I found out about them and why you married me, I was hurt and angry. I wanted some sort of revenge, I suppose. I decided to make you believe I'd married you for the same reason. I lied to you.'

'Why did you marry me, then?' Gil asked quietly.

She might as well be honest about that as well. 'I loved you. It's as simple as that.'

She trembled as she made the admission and Gil reached across and took her hand in his. 'Susannah lied to you, Olivia. Yes, I own twenty per cent of the company's shares. Vivien gave them to me five years ago. She said they should have gone to Philip, but since he had died she wanted me to have them. In the circumstances, I couldn't refuse. Not many people knew because we both agreed it would be better if they were held in the name of a representative rather than my own to prevent any speculation that I wanted to merge Beaufort's with Rossaro Advertising. Vivien knew I wouldn't do that. So you see, Olivia, they had nothing to do with our marriage.'

Olivia wished she could believe him but there were still too many unanswered questions. 'If they had nothing to do with our marriage, why didn't you tell me about them beforehand? Why weren't you honest with me?' she demanded.

Gil's grip on her hand tightened. 'I didn't tell you because I was worried you would think exactly that—that they had something to do with my marrying you. I planned to tell you after the wedding but then you dropped your bombshell and I thought you'd known about them all along.'

Olivia frowned, as if she'd found something he'd said strange. 'You said the shares had nothing to do with why you married me.'

'That's right.'

'Then why did you . . . marry me, I mean?'

'Don't you know? Can't you guess? I love you too, Olivia.'

She stared at him then, searching his face for some sign that he was making fun of her. How could he love her? He'd slept with Susannah on the eve of their wedding. Unless . . . unless Susannah had lied about that too. 'Susannah said something else as well,' she said quietly.

'What?'

'She . . . she said you and she had slept together the night before our wedding.'

There was an explosive silence then Gil ground out, 'The bitch! And you believed her?'

'I didn't want to. But so many of the things she said seemed to make sense. You'd been so cold and distant towards me all week, as if you regretted asking me to marry you at all. And that night, when I telephoned the hotel, they told me you'd had dinner with Susannah the night before. Just you and Susannah alone. Brad wasn't there.'

'Brad wasn't there because he dropped out at the last minute. He wasn't feeling well. No one was more surprised than me when I arrived and found Susannah waiting alone. Refusing to dine with her would have seemed churlish. By God, I wish I had now.'

'So... so you didn't sleep with her?'

Gil's eyes glittered, as if he found even the suggestion offensive. 'Of course I didn't. Whatever there was between Susannah and me was over long ago; I told you that. We had contact through work but that was all. I told her I wasn't interested in anything else. I thought she'd accepted that it was over between us but obviously she hadn't. She knew the worst way of paying me back was to hurt you and that's what she did.'

Suddenly Gil was pulling her up into his arms and holding her very tight. 'Believe me, Olivia. There was nothing between Susannah and me. There hadn't been for a long time.'

Olivia felt herself trembling all over. The pressure of Gil's body against hers was making her feel incredibly weak, and more than anything she wanted to lean against him, to take strength from his strength.

She did believe him. She knew now that she'd been wrong about a lot of things. Gil wasn't capable of the despicable behaviour Susannah had described. She should have known that. Perhaps she had known it deep inside but her own fear of being hurt had made her put up a defensive barrier and prevented her from seeing the truth.

Gil stared down at her, his eyes suddenly dark and very, very serious. 'I love you, Olivia. I think I started to fall in love with you five years ago, only I wouldn't admit it.'

'Five years ago?'

Gil nodded. 'I know it probably didn't look that way at the time. When I found you with that boy that night, I was half blind with jealousy. I told myself it was a moral anger but it wasn't. I was jealous. Jealous as hell. For the past five years I couldn't get you out of my mind. Oh, yes, I saw other women...had relationships with some of them...but it was always you my thoughts kept coming back to. I took the MD's job with Beaufort's because I knew I had to sort out my feelings for you once and for all. Even then I wouldn't admit my need for you. I knew I wanted you in a way I'd never wanted any other woman but I wouldn't call that wanting love. I tried to give it any other name but that one. But I can't deny it any longer. I love you, Olivia.'

'Gil, there's something I should tell you... While you were away, I found out I'm not pregnant. Does it make any difference?'

Gil pulled her into his arms and held her close. 'It's you I want...you I love.'

'But if I had been pregnant?'

'I'd have loved our baby too.'

'Oh, Gil! So would I. When I found out I was disappointed. I suddenly realised how much I wanted your baby.'

His hand curved possessively on her abdomen and he gave a husky laugh. 'I don't think that should be too difficult to arrange.'

Olivia smiled with mock innocence. 'But you look exhausted. Don't you want to rest?'

Gil shook his head. 'Making babies sounds like much more fun.'

He took her hand and led her towards the stairs. She followed willingly. 'Mrs McDonald will be pleased,' she murmured, as they reached the top.

'What has Mrs McDonald got to do with it?' Gil demanded, reaching for her.

Olivia smiled softly. 'She thinks the house needs children.'

Gil pulled her to him. 'Right now, I need you.'

The eager response of her kiss told him just how much she needed him too.

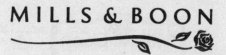

MILLS & BOON

EXCITING NEW COVERS

To reflect the ever-changing contemporary romance series we've designed new covers which perfectly capture the warmth, glamour and sophistication of modern-day romantic situations.

We know, because we've designed them with your comments in mind, that you'll just love the bright, warm, romantic colours and the up-to-date new look.

WATCH OUT FOR THESE NEW COVERS

From October 1993   Price £1.80

Proudly present to you...

BETTY NEELS' 100TH ROMANCE

Betty has been writing for Mills & Boon Romances for over 20 years. She began once she had retired from her job as a Ward Sister. She is married to a Dutchman and spent many years in Holland. Both her experiences as a nurse and her knowledge and love of Holland feature in many of her novels.

Her latest romance *'AT ODDS WITH LOVE'* is available from August 1993, price £1.80.

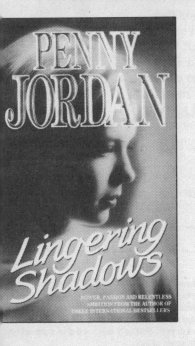

Accept 4 FREE Romances and 2 FREE gifts

FROM READER SERVICE

Here's an irresistible invitation from Mills & Boon. Please accept our offer of 4 FREE Romances, a CUDDLY TEDDY and a special MYSTERY GIFT! Then, if you choose, go on to enjoy 6 captivating Romances every month for just £1.80 each, postage and packing FREE. Plus our FREE Newsletter with author news, competitions and much more.

Send the coupon below to: Mills & Boon Reader Service, FREEPOST, PO Box 236, Croydon, Surrey CR9 9EL.

NO STAMP REQUIRED

Yes! Please rush me 4 FREE Romances and 2 FREE gifts! Please also reserve me a Reader Service subscription. If I decide to subscribe I can look forward to receiving 6 brand new Romances for just £10.80 each month, post and packing FREE. If I decide not to subscribe I shall write to you within 10 days - I can keep the free books and gifts whatever I choose. I may cancel or suspend my subscription at any time. I am over 18 years of age.

Ms/Mrs/Miss/Mr _____ EP55R

Address _____

_____

Postcode _____ Signature _____

Next Month's Romances

Each month you can choose from a wide variety of romance with Mills & Boon. Below are the new titles to look out for next month, why not ask either Mills & Boon Reader Service or your Newsagent to reserve you a copy of the titles you want to buy – just tick the titles you would like and either post to Reader Service or take it to any Newsagent and ask them to order your books.

Please save me the following titles:	Please tick	√
THE WEDDING	Emma Darcy	
LOVE WITHOUT REASON	Alison Fraser	
FIRE IN THE BLOOD	Charlotte Lamb	
GIVE A MAN A BAD NAME	Roberta Leigh	
TRAVELLING LIGHT	Sandra Field	
A HEALING FIRE	Patricia Wilson	
AN OLD ENCHANTMENT	Amanda Browning	
STRANGERS BY DAY	Vanessa Grant	
CONSPIRACY OF LOVE	Stephanie Howard	
FIERY ATTRACTION	Emma Richmond	
RESCUED	Rachel Elliot	
DEFIANT LOVE	Jessica Hart	
BOGUS BRIDE	Elizabeth Duke	
ONE SHINING SUMMER	Quinn Wilder	
TRUST TOO MUCH	Jayne Bauling	
A TRUE MARRIAGE	Lucy Gordon	

If you would like to order these books in addition to your regular subscription from Mills & Boon Reader Service please send £1.80 per title to: Mills & Boon Reader Service, Freepost, P.O. Box 236, Croydon, Surrey, CR9 9EL, quote your Subscriber No:.................................... (If applicable) and complete the name and address details below. Alternatively, these books are available from many local Newsagents including W.H.Smith, J.Menzies, Martins and other paperback stockists from 10 September 1993.

Name:..

Address:..

....Post Code:..........................

To Retailer: If you would like to stock M&B books please contact your regular book/magazine wholesaler for details.

You may be mailed with offers from other reputable companies as a result of this application. If you would rather not take advantage of these opportunities please tick box ☐